NOURISHMENT FOR THE SOUL

Volume I

Clarence R Wallace

Scan the QR to stay connected for news and updates!

Dedication

To: _______________________________

From: _______________________________

Acknowledgment

I must first acknowledge God for allowing me the privilege of authoring this book. As the Bible states in Psalm 68:11, "The Lord gave the word: great was the company of those that published it."

I want to thank my mother, Erline Wallace, who inspired me to become the man I am today. Her fighting spirit, unwavering determination, love, and resilience have always been my guiding light. Yes, she is my hero. Bless her soul. To my dad, Noel Wallace, while we didn't spend much time together, the moments we shared were precious. His look of love and pride when he saw me spoke volumes. He was a kind soul.

To my eldest sister, Rema, who paved the way for my mom, my twin sister Lyneve, and I to migrate to Canada from Jamaica, I say thank you. Rema was a fighter and always focused on what she wanted out of life.

To my son, Johnathan Wallace, I love how focused you are on achieving your goals and your no-nonsense demeanor. Love you.

To the rest of my family and friends who are too numerous to mention, you all inspire me in your own unique ways. That's cool!

To Derick Ellis, my prayer partner during early mornings and at other times of the day, much love and blessings. Your labor of love is much appreciated.

To the City of Brampton and the Black Economic Empowerment Department, I am grateful for your partnership in hosting the launch of the first edition of this book at City Hall. I am honored to have received this opportunity.

To my faithful supporter, Beheshta, and the staff at RBC, thank you for your engagement, encouragement, and support during one of the most difficult periods of my life. Beheshta, you are the real deal, my friend.

Thank you to everyone who assisted in making this a reality. Real Reel Reality!

To Jenna West, Sam Miller, and the team at KDP Publisher, who worked with Jake and I to see this book to its completion, I say thank you.

This book would not have been completed in the time it was without the effort and cooperation of so many individuals. I also want to thank those who resisted my purpose in life. Thank you for diverting me to my destiny. Evil intentions can lead to your ascension. Remember Joseph, whose brothers put him in the pit, and Potiphar's wife, Zuleikha, who lied about him, leading to his imprisonment and later his ascension to the office of the Prime Minister of Egypt.

Last but not least, Jake Ellis Kuria, my Kenyan son. Imagine a Kenyan and Jamaican combination—Kenyan controls the distance, and Jamaican the sprint. That's ultimate dominance.

Jake's professionalism, work ethic, loyalty, and team spirit are off the charts. The synergistic effects of our mindset and skillset are something I've never experienced before. There is a chapter dedicated to Jake in this book. Thank you for your faithfulness, belief, and commitment to the vision. By the grace of God, we did it. The best is yet to come, my son.

Contents

Preface

In the hustle and bustle of our modern lives, amidst the clamor for success and the pursuit of material wealth, it's easy to overlook the most essential aspect of our existence: the nourishment of the soul. In Nourishment For The Soul: Quotes He Wrote, Clarence R Wallace invites readers on a transformative journey to explore the profound significance of nurturing our innermost selves.

Wallace opens the discourse with a poignant reflection on the greatest hunger from which people perish, the hunger of an empty soul, devoid of joy, love, and tranquility. Through his insightful prose, he illuminates the timeless wisdom encapsulated in scripture, particularly in Mark 8:35-37, underscoring the paramount importance of prioritizing spiritual nourishment over worldly pursuits.

Drawing upon a rich tapestry of real-life experiences, Wallace weaves together a compelling narrative that vividly contrasts the fleeting allure of material wealth with the enduring richness of the soul. From the cautionary tale of the successful businessman ensnared by the trappings of prosperity to the inspiring example of the selfless individual dedicated to serving others, each anecdote serves as a poignant reminder of the immeasurable value of the soul.

As readers journey through the pages of this book, they are invited to reflect deeply on their own lives and choices, to consider what truly matters amidst the clamor of modernity. Through Wallace's eloquent prose and profound insights, they are empowered to embark on a quest for spiritual fulfillment, to cultivate virtues such as love, compassion, and inner peace that nourish the soul and imbue life with purpose and meaning.

In conclusion, Nourishment for the Soul: Quotes He Wrote serves as a timeless beacon of wisdom in an increasingly chaotic world. It beckons readers to heed the call to feed their souls, to embrace the profound truth that the satisfaction of the soul is worth more than any earthly riches. With each turn of the page, may readers find inspiration, solace, and guidance on their journey toward lasting fulfillment and true abundance.

Chapter 1

Nourishing the Soul

A Path to Fulfillment

"The greatest hunger from which people perish is the hunger of an empty soul, devoid of joy, love, and tranquility. Those who suffer from soul hunger are more easily angered than those suffering from an empty stomach.

Take time to feed your soul; it's more precious than a cold, lifeless piece of gold. Satisfaction of the soul is worth more than a treasure chest filled with gold. A fulfilled soul has the ability to unearth gold and, in doing so, attain its goal."

C R Wallace

The greatest hunger from which people perish is the hunger of an empty soul, devoid of joy, love, and tranquility. This concept resonates with the scripture verse from Mark 8:35-37, which speaks to the value of the soul over worldly gain. In verse 35, Jesus teaches that those who prioritize their own worldly desires will ultimately lose their life, while those who are willing to lose their life for His sake and the gospel will find true salvation. This emphasizes the importance of prioritizing spiritual nourishment over material pursuits.

Consider the example of a successful businessman who accumulates vast wealth and possessions but neglects the well-being of his soul. He has achieved remarkable financial success, owning luxurious homes, driving expensive cars, and enjoying the finest things money can buy. On the surface, his life appears enviable, filled with material abundance and the trappings of success. However, beneath this exterior lies a profound emptiness and lack of fulfillment. Despite his outward achievements, he feels a void that money cannot fill, a persistent sense of dissatisfaction and inner turmoil.

This scenario echoes the sentiment of Mark 8:36, where Jesus asks, "For what shall it profit a man, if he shall gain the whole world, and lose his own soul?" The question challenges us to consider the true value of material success in relation to the state of our soul. It serves as a poignant reminder that no amount of worldly wealth or possessions can compensate for the loss of one's soul. The businessman's story illustrates this truth vividly, showing that even with immense wealth, one can still feel incomplete and unfulfilled if the soul is neglected.

True fulfillment, as the teachings of Jesus highlight, comes from nurturing the soul with qualities like joy, love, and tranquility. These qualities are not found in material possessions but are cultivated through spiritual practices, meaningful relationships, and a life aligned with higher values and purpose. Joy arises from a deep sense of gratitude and contentment, love from genuine connections with others, and tranquility from inner peace and a clear conscience.

For the businessman, the path to true fulfillment might involve re-evaluating his priorities and making time for spiritual growth. This could mean engaging in practices like meditation, prayer, or reflection, which help connect him to his inner self and to God. It might also involve fostering deeper relationships with family and friends, giving back to the community, and finding ways to serve others. By doing so, he can begin to fill the void that material wealth alone cannot satisfy, experiencing a sense of wholeness and peace that comes from a well-nurtured soul.

In essence, the lesson here is that while worldly achievements can bring temporary satisfaction, they cannot substitute for the deeper, lasting fulfillment that comes from caring for the soul. By focusing on qualities like joy, love, and tranquility, we can achieve a sense of true success that encompasses both our external accomplishments and our inner well-being.

In contrast, let's look at an individual who dedicates their life to serving others and living in accordance with spiritual principles. This person might not have accumulated great wealth or fame, but their soul is enriched with qualities that bring lasting fulfillment.

Their days are filled with acts of kindness, compassion, and selflessness. They find joy in helping those in need, in offering a listening ear, and in being a source of comfort and support to others. Their life is a testament to the profound satisfaction that comes from living a purpose-driven and spiritually aligned existence.

This aligns with the message of Mark 8:37, which asks, "Or what shall a man give in exchange for his soul?" The question highlights the incomparable value of the soul, emphasizing that no material possession or worldly achievement can replace its worth. The soul's value is immeasurable, transcending the fleeting nature of earthly riches and status.

The individual who lives in service to others embodies this principle. Though they may not be recognized by society's standards of success, their life is rich with meaning and purpose. Their soul, nourished by love, compassion, and inner peace, radiates a sense of fulfillment that far surpasses the temporary pleasures of material wealth. They experience a deep connection with others, a sense of belonging, and a profound inner tranquility that arises from knowing they are living in alignment with their higher self and divine principles.

Therefore, it is essential for individuals to prioritize nourishing their souls by cultivating virtues such as love, compassion, and inner peace. This soul nourishment is more precious than any material wealth, as it brings true fulfillment and leads to a life of purpose and meaning. To nurture the soul, one might engage in practices like meditation, prayer, and self-reflection, which help to cultivate a deeper awareness of one's inner self and connection to the divine.

Additionally, engaging in acts of service and kindness can significantly enrich the soul. Volunteering, supporting friends and family, and showing empathy towards others are all ways to strengthen the qualities that bring lasting fulfillment. These actions not only benefit those who receive help but also deeply nourish the giver's soul, fostering a sense of interconnectedness and shared humanity.

In essence, the true measure of a fulfilling life is not found in the accumulation of wealth or accolades, but in the quality of one's soul. By focusing on spiritual growth and the cultivation of virtues, individuals can achieve a deeper, more enduring sense of fulfillment. The soul, when enriched with love, compassion, and peace, provides a foundation for a meaningful and purpose-driven life, far surpassing the ephemeral satisfaction of material success.

Therefore, it's essential for individuals to prioritize nourishing their souls by cultivating virtues such as love, compassion, and inner peace. This soul nourishment is more precious than any material wealth, as it brings true fulfillment and leads to a life of purpose and meaning.

Cultivating love involves fostering deep, genuine connections with others. This means showing kindness, patience, and understanding in our relationships. Acts of love can be as simple as offering a comforting word to a friend in distress, volunteering at a local shelter, or spending quality time with family. Love nourishes the soul by creating a sense of belonging and mutual respect, enriching our lives with emotional warmth and security.

Compassion, on the other hand, is the empathy and concern we show for the suffering of others. It requires us to step outside of our own experiences and consider the feelings and challenges faced by those around us. Practicing compassion can transform our interactions and society at large, fostering an environment where people feel seen, heard, and valued. Compassionate acts, such as helping a neighbor in need or supporting charitable causes, deepen our sense of connection to the human family and cultivate a soul rich in kindness and empathy.

Inner peace is the tranquility that arises from a well-balanced and centered mind. Achieving inner peace involves practices that calm the mind and spirit, such as meditation, prayer, and mindfulness. These practices help us to manage stress, reduce anxiety, and find clarity in the midst of life's chaos. Inner peace allows us to approach life's challenges with a calm and composed demeanor, making thoughtful decisions that align with our values and spiritual beliefs. Together, these virtues create a foundation for a deeply fulfilling life. They guide us to live authentically, with a focus on what truly matters beyond the superficial and material aspects of existence. Prioritizing the nourishment of the soul through love, compassion, and inner peace leads to lasting happiness and contentment. This holistic approach to life enables us to find joy in everyday moments, appreciate the beauty of simple acts of kindness, and maintain a sense of purpose and direction.

Moreover, the benefits of soul nourishment extend beyond the individual. A person who embodies these virtues positively impacts their community and the wider world. Their actions inspire others to also pursue a path of love and compassion, creating a ripple effect that fosters a more caring and harmonious society. In this way, the pursuit of soul nourishment contributes to a collective upliftment, where the well-being of each person enhances the well-being of all.

In conclusion, nourishing the soul by cultivating love, compassion, and inner peace is crucial for achieving true fulfillment. This form of wealth, unlike material possessions, endures and enriches every aspect of our lives, leading to a profound sense of purpose and meaning. By focusing on these virtues, we not only enhance our own lives but also contribute to a better, more compassionate world.

Life experiences that illustrate the importance of nourishing the soul:

1. Sacrificing Self for Fulfillment:

Consider a person who is deeply passionate about their career but finds themselves consumed by ambition, sacrificing relationships and personal well-being for professional success. They devote countless hours to their job, striving for promotions, recognition, and financial rewards. However, despite achieving these milestones, they experience a lingering sense of emptiness and spiritual hunger. Their life, defined by worldly achievements, lacks deeper meaning and fulfillment.

This scenario reflects the teachings of Mark 8:35, where Jesus says, "For whoever wants to save their life will lose it, but whoever loses their life for me and for the gospel will save it." The message encourages individuals to shift their focus from self-centered ambitions to values that align with serving others and spiritual growth.

The transformative journey begins when this person starts to prioritize values such as love, compassion, and service over personal gain. They may begin to volunteer in their community, engage in meaningful conversations with loved ones, or support causes that align with their principles. By relinquishing their self-centered desires and embracing a life centered on serving others and fostering spiritual growth, they start to experience a profound transformation.

As they invest time and energy into helping others and building meaningful relationships, they find a sense of purpose and fulfillment that their career alone could not provide. Their life becomes enriched with joy, love, and inner peace. They discover that true fulfillment comes from giving of oneself and living according to higher principles.

This transformation echoes the scriptural message of losing one's life to save it. By letting go of their former identity, rooted in worldly achievements and self-interest, they gain a new life characterized by spiritual richness and deep satisfaction. Their journey serves as a powerful reminder that true success and fulfillment are found not in accumulating material wealth or accolades, but in cultivating a life of purpose, love, and service.

In essence, the story illustrates that by sacrificing self-centered ambitions and embracing a life dedicated to spiritual growth and service to others, individuals can find true fulfillment. This profound shift aligns with biblical teachings and highlights the enduring value of living a life rooted in compassion, love, and inner peace. Through this transformation, they save their life in the truest sense, discovering a deeper, more meaningful existence that transcends the superficial rewards of worldly success.

2. Wealth and Soul Enrichment:

Imagine someone dedicating their life to accumulating wealth, pursuing material possessions and worldly pleasures at the expense of their spiritual well-being. They invest their time and energy in building a fortune, acquiring luxury homes, expensive cars, and other symbols of success. On the surface, they appear to have everything one could desire. However, despite amassing great riches, they feel a profound sense of inner emptiness and discontent. The constant pursuit of more leaves them spiritually malnourished, and their life lacks the deeper fulfillment that comes from nurturing the soul.

This scenario vividly illustrates the warning found in Mark 8:36, where Jesus asks, "For what shall it profit a man, if he shall gain the whole world, and lose his own soul?" The scripture underscores the futility of gaining material wealth at the cost of one's spiritual health. It serves as a poignant reminder that no amount of worldly success can compensate for the loss of one's soul, highlighting the intrinsic value of spiritual well-being over material accumulation.

Conversely, consider another individual who chooses to prioritize nourishing their soul through acts of kindness, generosity, and spiritual practices. This person may not possess vast material wealth, but their life is rich with experiences and qualities that bring deep fulfillment. They find joy in giving to others, whether through time, resources, or simple acts of kindness. Their daily practices might include meditation, prayer, or engaging in community service, all of which contribute to a deep sense of inner peace and contentment.

Their soul becomes a treasure far more valuable than any worldly riches. The richness of their spirit is evident in their interactions with others; they exude compassion, empathy, and a genuine sense of happiness that material wealth alone cannot provide. They experience a connection to something greater than themselves, finding purpose and meaning in their actions and relationships.

This enriched state of being aligns with the scriptural emphasis on the importance of the soul over material possessions. By prioritizing spiritual growth and the well-being of others, they embody the true essence of fulfillment. Their life serves as a testament to the enduring value of virtues like love, compassion, and inner peace, which contribute to a sense of wholeness and satisfaction that transcends the temporary pleasure of material wealth.

In essence, the contrast between these two individuals underscores a vital truth: while the pursuit of wealth and material success can lead to a hollow existence, focusing on the enrichment of the soul through virtuous living offers a profound and lasting fulfill-ment. The individual who chooses to nourish their soul discovers a depth of happiness and contentment that far exceeds the fleeting re-wards of worldly riches. Their life reflects the timeless wisdom that true wealth is measured not by material possessions, but by the rich-ness of the spirit and the quality of one's inner life.

3. Value of Spiritual Currency:

Reflect on the concept of exchanging one's soul for worldly gain. In today's society, many people chase after fame, power, or temporary pleasures, often compromising their integrity and values in the process. Yet, when faced with the question posed in the scrip-ture—what shall a man give in exchange for his soul, they realize that no amount of worldly success or temporary pleasures can com-pensate for the loss of spiritual fulfillment and inner peace. Priori-tizing the nourishment of the soul through spiritual practices, mean-ingful relationships, and acts of service becomes paramount in main-taining a balanced and fulfilling life.

Incorporating these scripture verses into real-life experi-ences underscores the timeless wisdom of prioritizing the nourish-ment of the soul over worldly pursuits. By aligning our lives with principles of love, compassion, and spiritual growth, we can culti-vate a sense of fulfillment that transcends material wealth and tem-poral pleasures, ultimately leading to a life of greater purpose and meaning.

4. Personal Experience:

"In my own journey, I've encountered opportunities for advancement, promotions, and salary increases within many organizations, promising not just financial growth but also a perceived elevation in status within both the company and society. However, I made a conscious decision not to compromise my principles and integrity for these superficial gains. This choice led to my alienation and, ultimately, the loss of my job. Despite facing adversity, I remained steadfast in my commitment to preserving my soul's integrity, recognizing its inherent value over the fleeting allure of wealth and societal recognition.

Amidst the turmoil, I found solace in the fact that I did not lose my soul in the pursuit of worldly success. This realization served as a profound reminder that true wealth lies not in material possessions but in the moral and spiritual richness of one's soul. It became evident that chasing after fool's gold, while neglecting the nourishment of the soul, is a hollow endeavor that ultimately leads to spiritual bankruptcy.

Choosing righteousness over material possessions has brought me a sense of peace that surpasses understanding and a love that transcends mere knowledge. Removed from the toxic environment that threatened to erode my soul's well-being, I've discovered a newfound freedom to pursue my purpose with ease, unburdened by the constraints of a soul-diseased workplace.

This personal journey underscores the timeless wisdom conveyed in the discourse on nourishing the soul. It serves as a testament to the importance of prioritizing spiritual nourishment over the transient allure of worldly pursuits, affirming that true fulfillment and abundance are found in the richness of the soul rather than the accumulation of material wealth."

As we journey forward, may we remember the timeless wisdom encapsulated in these words and strive to nourish our souls, for therein lies the path to lasting fulfillment and true abundance.

Conclusion:

In the exploration of nourishing the soul as a path to fulfillment, we've delved into the profound truth that the hunger of an empty soul, devoid of joy, love, and tranquility, surpasses the perils of physical deprivation. Rooted in the scripture verse from Mark 8:35-37, we've witnessed the invaluable wisdom of prioritizing spiritual nourishment over the allure of worldly gain.

Through real-life examples and personal experiences, we've seen the stark contrast between those who chase after material wealth at the expense of their soul's well-being and those who prioritize spiritual growth and service to others. It's become evident that true fulfillment emanates from nurturing the soul with qualities like love, compassion, and inner peace, transcending the temporary pleasures of material possessions.

As we move forward on our individual journeys, let us heed the call to feed our souls, recognizing that the satisfaction of the soul is worth more than any amount of gold or earthly riches. May we prioritize spiritual nourishment, cultivate virtues, and align our lives with principles of love and compassion, for therein lies the path to lasting fulfillment and true abundance.

Key Points:

1. The Greatest Hunger:

The chapter highlights that the most perilous hunger is that of an empty soul, lacking joy, love, and tranquility, which can lead to greater suffering than physical hunger.

2. Value of Spiritual Nourishment:

Spiritual nourishment is emphasized over material pursuits, drawing from the scripture verse from Mark 8:35-37, emphasizing the importance of prioritizing the soul's well-being.

3. Contrast in Priorities:

The chapter contrasts the pursuit of material wealth with the enrichment of the soul, showcasing examples of individuals who prioritize worldly success over spiritual fulfillment.

4. Essential Virtues:

It stresses the importance of cultivating virtues such as love, compassion, and inner peace for nourishing the soul, which brings true fulfillment and leads to a meaningful life.

5. Real-life Examples:

Through personal experiences and anecdotes, the chapter illustrates the contrast between those who prioritize material wealth and those who prioritize spiritual growth, highlighting the richness of spirit that transcends material possessions.

6. Value of the Soul:

It emphasizes the immeasurable worth of the soul, suggesting that no material possession or worldly achievement can replace its value.

7. Call to Action:

The chapter urges readers to prioritize soul nourishment, aligning their lives with principles of love, compassion, and spiritual growth for lasting fulfillment and true abundance.

8. Conclusion:

The conclusion reiterates the importance of feeding the soul, recognizing its intrinsic value over material possessions, and encourages readers to embark on a journey of spiritual nourishment for a meaningful and fulfilling life.

Chapter 2

The Billionaire Mindset

Rethinking Wealth Accumulation

"Reset your mindset for the manifestation of wealth generation. A billionaire mindset understands that a billion dollars is not solely defined by what's in their bank accounts or stock portfolio. Their billions are temporarily held in other people's accounts, awaiting transfer through transactions. It's that simple, believe me. Transactions lead to a life of satisfaction. Stop reacting and start planning to make transactions."

C R Wallace

I had a conversation with a bank manager at an event where I mentioned that I am a billionaire. His immediate response was, "I need to hang with you." I asked him if he was a billionaire himself, to which he replied, "No, I'm not." I then questioned him further, asking if he would carry a billion dollars in his wallet if he were a billionaire. His response was, "No, it would be in various investments."

I took the opportunity to explain to him that I also don't carry a billion dollars in my wallet. Instead, I informed him that the billions are securely held in other people's accounts, awaiting transactions to transfer them into my own account. This conversation led me to reflect on the biblical wisdom found in Proverbs 13:22, which emphasizes leaving an inheritance for future generations and suggests that the wealth of the unjust eventually benefits the righteous.

The quote "The Billionaire Mindset: Rethinking Wealth Accumulation" encapsulates a powerful concept that challenges traditional notions of wealth and encourages a shift in mindset towards proactive wealth generation. Let's explore this idea further with real-life examples:

1. Entrepreneurial Ventures:

Many successful entrepreneurs embody the billionaire mindset by focusing on creating value and seizing opportunities for growth. This mindset goes beyond accumulating wealth through traditional investments; it involves leveraging resources, networks, and innovative ideas to build thriving businesses. Entrepreneurs with this mindset are often characterized by their ability to identify gaps in the market and develop solutions that meet those needs in unique and transformative ways.

For example, Elon Musk, the CEO of SpaceX and Tesla, didn't accumulate his wealth solely through traditional investments but through ambitious ventures that revolutionized industries. Musk's approach to entrepreneurship is marked by his willingness to tackle high-risk, high-reward projects. With SpaceX, he aimed to reduce the cost of space travel and make it possible for humans to live on other planets, a goal that was previously considered unattainable. Similarly, with Tesla, Musk sought to accelerate the world's transition to sustainable energy, creating electric vehicles that compete with traditional gasoline-powered cars in performance and appeal.

Musk's success is not just due to his innovative ideas but also his ability to execute those ideas effectively. He has built strong teams, fostered a culture of relentless innovation, and maintained a long-term vision despite numerous challenges. His ventures have not only disrupted existing industries but also created entirely new markets, demonstrating the power of a billionaire mindset focused on creating substantial and lasting value.

This mindset is also evident in other entrepreneurs like Jeff Bezos, founder of Amazon, and Sara Blakely, founder of Spanx. Bezos transformed the retail industry by leveraging the internet to create an unparalleled shopping experience, while Blakely revolutionized the undergarment industry with her innovative products and persistent approach. Both have built empires by continuously seeking out new opportunities for growth and improvement, underscoring the importance of vision, resilience, and adaptability in entrepreneurial success.

2. Strategic Investments:

Billionaires understand the power of strategic investments beyond the stock market. They diversify their portfolios by investing in real estate, startups, and other high-yield opportunities, recognizing that a well-rounded investment strategy can mitigate risks and maximize returns. These investments often involve more than just capital; they include providing guidance, leveraging networks, and sometimes actively participating in the management of these ventures.

For instance, Warren Buffett, often hailed as one of the greatest investors of all time, built his fortune through shrewd investments in undervalued companies and long-term growth strategies. Buffett's investment philosophy is centered on value investing, where he identifies companies with strong fundamentals that are temporarily undervalued by the market. He looks for businesses with a durable competitive advantage, competent management, and predictable earnings. By holding these investments for the long term, Buffett has been able to capitalize on their growth and weather market volatility.

Buffett's investment in Coca-Cola is a prime example. When many investors were skeptical about the future of the beverage industry, Buffett saw an opportunity in Coca-Cola's global brand and consistent earnings. His decision to invest heavily in Coca-Cola during the late 1980s has paid off immensely, proving the effectiveness of his long-term approach.

Beyond stocks, billionaires like Buffett also invest in real estate, which can provide stable cash flows and appreciate over time. Real estate investments range from commercial properties to luxury residences and large tracts of land. These investments not only diversify their portfolios but also provide tangible assets that can generate passive income.

Additionally, billionaires frequently invest in start-ups and venture capital opportunities. These high-risk, high-reward investments can lead to significant returns if the start-up succeeds. For example, early investments in tech companies like Facebook, Uber, and Airbnb have yielded substantial returns for those who recognized their potential early on. Billionaires often use their expertise and networks to mentor and support these start-ups, increasing the likelihood of their success.

In conclusion, the strategic investment approach of billionaires like Warren Buffett exemplifies the importance of diversification, patience, and the ability to recognize and act on high-potential opportunities. By spreading their investments across various asset classes and sectors, they not only enhance their financial security but also open doors to new and lucrative ventures.

3. Philanthropic Endeavors:

True wealth goes beyond financial abundance; it includes making a positive impact on society. Many billionaires channel their resources towards philanthropic endeavors that address social issues and improve the lives of others. These philanthropic efforts often aim to tackle systemic problems, providing solutions that have far-reaching and sustainable impacts.

For instance, Priscilla Chan and Mark Zuckerberg established the Chan Zuckerberg Initiative (CZI), one of the most ambitious and impactful philanthropic organizations in the world. CZI focuses on personalized learning, curing diseases, connecting people, and building strong communities, demonstrating how wealth can be used to create lasting change. The initiative has been instrumental in advancing medical research, particularly in areas like neuroscience and rare diseases, through substantial funding for scientific research and technology development. Additionally, CZI works to improve educational outcomes by supporting personalized learning and providing resources to underserved schools and communities. By leveraging their resources and influence, Chan and Zuckerberg aim to address some of the most pressing challenges of our time and drive transformative progress across various sectors.

Another example is Warren Buffett, who has pledged to give

away the majority of his fortune to philanthropic causes. In 2006, Buffett announced his decision to donate 85% of his Berkshire Hathaway shares to five charitable foundations, with the largest portion going to the Gates Foundation. This commitment underscores the belief that wealth should be used to benefit society, particularly in addressing urgent global challenges.

Other billionaires, such as Michael Bloomberg and MacKenzie Scott, have also made significant philanthropic contributions. Bloomberg, through his Bloomberg Philanthropies, has focused on public health, climate change, education, and the arts. His contributions have supported anti-tobacco campaigns, climate resilience projects, and educational reforms, showcasing a comprehensive approach to philanthropy.

MacKenzie Scott has taken a unique approach to philanthropy by providing large, unrestricted grants to various organizations, allowing them the flexibility to use the funds where they are most needed. Her donations have supported racial equity, public health, and economic mobility. Scott's approach emphasizes trust in non-profit organizations to make the best use of the resources provided, fostering innovation and responsiveness in addressing social issues.

Philanthropic endeavors by billionaires not only address immediate needs but also aim to create systemic change. These efforts reflect a commitment to using wealth responsibly and ethically, ensuring that the benefits of their success extend beyond their personal and business achievements. By investing in the well-being of communities and tackling global challenges, these philanthropists demonstrate that true wealth includes the capacity to improve the world for future generations.

4. Networking and Relationships:

Building strong relationships and strategic partnerships is another hallmark of the billionaire mindset. Successful individuals understand the value of collaboration and leverage their networks to unlock new opportunities, recognizing that no one achieves monumental success alone. The ability to connect with the right people can open doors to resources, knowledge, and opportunities that might otherwise remain inaccessible.

Oprah Winfrey is a prime example of how powerful networking and relationship-building can be. Winfrey built her media empire by cultivating relationships with influential figures and forming strategic alliances that propelled her career forward. From her early days in television to becoming a media mogul, Winfrey's connections with industry leaders, celebrities, and business executives played a crucial role in her success. Her ability to engage with diverse groups of people has helped her create a brand that resonates with a wide audience and establish partnerships that amplify her impact.

Another example is Richard Branson, the founder of the Virgin Group. Branson's business strategy heavily relies on forming strategic partnerships and leveraging his extensive network. By collaborating with various stakeholders across different industries, Branson has been able to expand the Virgin brand into sectors ranging from music and airlines to space travel. His personable approach and focus on building lasting relationships have been key to negotiating deals and launching successful ventures.

Similarly, Jeff Bezos, the founder of Amazon, has effectively utilized networking to grow his business. Bezos' ability to forge strong relationships with suppliers, business partners, and investors has been instrumental in Amazon's rise. His strategic alliances with companies like Apple, Google, and major retailers have helped Amazon become a dominant force in e-commerce and cloud computing.

Networking is not just about forming business partnerships; it's also about mentorship and learning. Many billionaires attribute their success to the guidance and advice they received from mentors and peers. For instance, Warren Buffett has often spoken about the influence of his mentor, Benjamin Graham, on his investment philosophy. Similarly, Mark Zuckerberg benefited from the mentorship of Steve Jobs and other tech industry veterans as he built Facebook.

The value of networking and relationships extends beyond immediate business gains. It fosters a collaborative environment where ideas can be exchanged, and innovation can thrive. Successful entrepreneurs understand that cultivating a robust network requires genuine engagement, trust, and mutual benefit. By building and maintaining strong relationships, they can access diverse perspectives, identify new opportunities, and create synergies that drive long-term success.

In summary, the ability to build and leverage strong relationships is a critical component of the billionaire mindset. Whether through strategic partnerships, mentorship, or collaborative ventures, successful individuals like Oprah Winfrey, Richard Branson, and Jeff Bezos demonstrate that networking is a powerful tool for unlocking potential and achieving remarkable success.

5. Innovation and Adaptability:

Billionaires embrace innovation and remain adaptable in the face of change. This ability to pivot and evolve is essential in a rapidly changing world where traditional industries can be disrupted by new technologies and shifting consumer preferences. By constantly seeking out new ways to add value and disrupt traditional models, successful entrepreneurs can stay ahead of the curve and sustain their growth.

Jeff Bezos, the founder of Amazon, exemplifies this mindset. Bezos transformed the retail landscape by pioneering e-commerce, a concept that revolutionized the way people shop. He started Amazon as an online bookstore, but his vision extended far beyond books. Recognizing the potential of the internet to reshape retail, Bezos expanded Amazon's offerings to include virtually every product category. This relentless drive to innovate didn't stop there. Bezos introduced Amazon Prime, a subscription service offering fast shipping and exclusive content, which significantly enhanced customer loyalty and transformed consumer expectations.

Amazon's innovation extends to logistics and technology as well. The company invested heavily in building a robust distribution network, including advanced warehouses and delivery systems. Bezos also ventured into cloud computing with Amazon Web Services (AWS), which became a major revenue stream and a market leader in the industry. AWS's success is a testament to Bezos's ability to recognize emerging trends and capitalize on them, fundamentally altering the tech landscape.

Another example of innovation and adaptability is Elon Musk, who continuously pushes the boundaries of what's possible across multiple industries. With Tesla, Musk not only popularized electric vehicles but also developed a comprehensive ecosystem that includes renewable energy solutions like solar panels and battery storage. His vision extends to autonomous driving technology, which has the potential to revolutionize transportation. Similarly, with SpaceX, Musk is redefining space exploration by developing reusable rockets, significantly reducing the cost of space travel and paving the way for future missions to Mars.

Sara Blakely, the founder of Spanx, also illustrates how innovation and adaptability can lead to monumental success. Blakely identified a gap in the market for comfortable and effective shapewear. Starting with a single product, she innovated within the apparel industry by focusing on design, comfort, and functionality. Her ability to adapt to consumer feedback and expand her product line has kept Spanx relevant and successful in a competitive market.

Innovation isn't limited to products and services; it also encompasses business models and strategies. Many successful entrepreneurs have disrupted their industries by rethinking how business is conducted. For example, Airbnb revolutionized the hospitality industry by creating a platform that connects travelers with private accommodations, offering a unique alternative to traditional hotels. This model has not only provided economic opportunities for hosts but also given travelers more options and personalized experiences.

6. Long-Term Vision:

The billionaire mindset is characterized by a focus on sustainable growth, long-lasting impact, and strategic planning. Instead of seeking short-term gains, billionaires invest in initiatives that promise enduring success and transformative effects on industries and society. This long-term perspective allows them to navigate challenges and capitalize on opportunities that others might overlook due to their more immediate concerns.

Mark Zuckerberg, the CEO of Facebook (now Meta), exemplifies this approach. Zuckerberg has consistently prioritized long-term innovation and expansion, driving the company's growth beyond its origins as a social media platform. Recognizing the limitations of relying solely on social networking, Zuckerberg has strategically invested in areas like virtual reality (VR) and artificial intelligence (AI). The acquisition of Oculus VR in 2014 marked a significant step towards building a future where immersive technologies play a central role in social interaction, gaming, and professional environments. This long-term vision is further evidenced by Meta's significant investment in the metaverse, aiming to create a virtual space that integrates VR, AR, and other advanced technologies.

Zuckerberg's approach underscores a commitment to staying ahead of technological trends and preparing for a future where digital experiences are more integrated into daily life. By investing in AI, Meta is enhancing its platforms with advanced capabilities such as improved content moderation, personalized user experiences, and new forms of interaction that can adapt to user needs in real-time. These initiatives are not about immediate returns but about positioning the company for continued relevance and leadership in the tech industry for decades to come.

Another example is Larry Page and Sergey Brin, the co-founders of Google (now Alphabet Inc.). From the beginning, Page and Brin envisioned Google as more than just a search engine. They invested in long-term projects such as autonomous vehicles through Waymo, life sciences through Verily, and smart city solutions through Sidewalk Labs. Alphabet's "moonshot" projects, managed under its research arm X, aim to address some of the world's biggest challenges, from renewable energy to global connectivity. These ventures often involve significant upfront investment with the understanding that the potential payoffs, both financially and societally, could be immense.

Similarly, Elon Musk's ventures, such as SpaceX and Tesla, are driven by long-term goals that go beyond immediate profitability. Musk's vision for SpaceX involves making space travel more affordable and eventually enabling human colonization of Mars. These ambitious objectives require sustained investment, innovation, and resilience in the face of setbacks. Tesla's mission to accelerate the world's transition to sustainable energy involves continuous development of electric vehicles, battery technology, and renewable energy solutions, with an eye on shaping the future of energy consumption and transportation.

The focus on long-term vision is not just about technological innovation but also about fostering a sustainable and impactful business model.

In conclusion, the billionaire mindset's emphasis on long-term vision and strategic planning is crucial for achieving sustainable growth and lasting impact. Leaders like Mark Zuckerberg, Larry Page, Sergey Brin and Elon Musk demonstrate that by looking beyond short-term gains and focusing on future possibilities, they can drive innovation, solve complex problems, and build enterprises that not only succeed but also contribute significantly to the advancement of society.

Mark Zuckerberg, the CEO of Facebook (now Meta), exemplifies this approach. Zuckerberg has consistently prioritized long-term innovation and expansion, driving the company's growth beyond its origins as a social media platform. Recognizing the limitations of relying solely on social networking, Zuckerberg has strategically invested in areas like virtual reality (VR) and artificial intelligence (AI). The acquisition of Oculus VR in 2014 marked a significant step towards building a future where immersive technologies play a central role in social interaction, gaming, and professional environments. This long-term vision is further evidenced by Meta's significant investment in the metaverse, aiming to create a virtual space that integrates VR, AR, and other advanced technologies.

Zuckerberg's approach underscores a commitment to staying ahead of technological trends and preparing for a future where digital experiences are more integrated into daily life. By investing in AI, Meta is enhancing its platforms with advanced capabilities such as improved content moderation, personalized user experiences, and new forms of interaction that can adapt to user needs in real-time. These initiatives are not about immediate returns but about positioning the company for continued relevance and leadership in the tech industry for decades to come.

Another example is Larry Page and Sergey Brin, the co-founders of Google (now Alphabet Inc.). From the beginning, Page and Brin envisioned Google as more than just a search engine. They invested in long-term projects such as autonomous vehicles through Waymo, life sciences through Verily, and smart city solutions through Sidewalk Labs. Alphabet's "moonshot" projects, managed under its research arm X, aim to address some of the world's biggest challenges, from renewable energy to global connectivity. These ventures often involve significant upfront investment with the understanding that the potential payoffs, both financially and societally, could be immense.

Similarly, Elon Musk's ventures, such as SpaceX and Tesla, are driven by long-term goals that go beyond immediate profitability. Musk's vision for SpaceX involves making space travel more affordable and eventually enabling human colonization of Mars. These ambitious objectives require sustained investment, innovation, and resilience in the face of setbacks. Tesla's mission to accelerate the world's transition to sustainable energy involves the continuous development of electric vehicles, battery technology, and renewable energy solutions, with an eye on shaping the future of energy consumption and transportation.

The focus on long-term vision is not just about technological innovation but also about fostering a sustainable and impactful business model. Bill Gates, through his work with the Bill and Melinda Gates Foundation, exemplifies this by addressing global health and development challenges. The foundation's investments in vaccine research, disease eradication, and education are designed to create lasting change, improving the quality of life for millions around the world.

In conclusion, the billionaire mindset's emphasis on long-term vision and strategic planning is crucial for achieving sustainable growth and lasting impact. Leaders like Mark Zuckerberg, Larry Page, Sergey Brin and Elon Musk demonstrate that by looking beyond short-term gains and focusing on future possibilities, they can drive innovation, solve complex problems, and build enterprises that not only succeed but also contribute significantly to the advancement of society.

Summary:

"The Billionaire Mindset: Rethinking Wealth Accumulation"

Resetting Your Mindset for Wealth Generation

A billionaire mindset redefines wealth, seeing it not just in terms of bank balances or stock portfolios but in the potential transactions that transfer wealth through innovative business ventures. This approach emphasizes proactive planning over reactive behavior to create value and satisfaction through transactions.

Illustrative Anecdote:

C R Wallace recounts a conversation with a bank manager, explaining that being a billionaire doesn't mean carrying vast sums of money but having wealth distributed in various investments and opportunities. This aligns with biblical wisdom that emphasizes the importance of strategic inheritance and wealth transfer.

Entrepreneurial Ventures:

Successful entrepreneurs create value and seize growth opportunities beyond traditional investments. Elon Musk's ventures with SpaceX and Tesla exemplify this, showing how innovative and high-risk projects can revolutionize industries and create significant wealth.

Strategic Investments:

Billionaires like Warren Buffett diversify their portfolios through strategic investments in undervalued companies, real estate, and startups. Buffett's long-term value investing, such as his investment in Coca-Cola, highlights the importance of patience and recognizing high-potential opportunities.

Philanthropic Endeavors:

Wealth also includes societal impact. Priscilla Chan and Mark Zuckerberg's Chan Zuckerberg Initiative (CZI) focuses on personalized learning, curing diseases, and building strong communities. Their substantial investments in scientific research and education demonstrate how wealth can drive lasting societal change.

Networking and Relationships:

Building strong relationships and strategic partnerships is crucial. Oprah Winfrey's media empire, built on influential connections, and Richard Branson's Virgin Group, grown through strategic alliances, illustrate how networking can unlock resources and opportunities.

Innovation and Adaptability:

Billionaires embrace change and innovation. Jeff Bezos's transformation of retail through Amazon and Elon Musk's ventures in electric vehicles and space travel shows how continuous innovation and adaptability can disrupt traditional industries and create new markets.

Long-Term Vision:

The billionaire mindset prioritizes long-term, sustainable growth. Mark Zuckerberg's investments in virtual reality and AI, Larry Page and Sergey Brin's "moonshot" projects with Alphabet, and Elon Musk's vision for affordable space travel and sustainable energy reflect a focus on future possibilities over immediate gains.

Conclusion:

The billionaire mindset's emphasis on long-term vision, innovation, strategic planning, and societal impact enables successful entrepreneurs to drive significant change, solve complex problems, and build enterprises that achieve lasting success and contribute to global advancement.

Key Points

1. Wealth Perception and Transactions:

A billionaire mindset views wealth as not just what's in their accounts but as money held in others' accounts, awaiting transactions.

Focus on planning for transactions instead of just reacting to circumstances.

2. Entrepreneurial Ventures:

Successful entrepreneurs like Elon Musk, Jeff Bezos, and Sara Blakely focus on creating value and seizing growth opportunities.

They innovate and tackle high-risk, high-reward projects, disrupting industries and creating new markets.

3. Strategic Investments:

Billionaires diversify their investments beyond traditional stocks into real estate, startups, and other high-yield opportunities. - They provide more than just capital, offering guidance and leveraging their networks.

4. Philanthropic Endeavors:

Wealth is also about making a positive societal impact

through philanthropy. Notable philanthropists like Warren Buffett, Priscilla Chan and, Mark Zuckerberg, and MacKenzie Scott address systemic issues and create sustainable impacts.

5. Networking and Relationships:

Building strong relationships and strategic partnerships is crucial. Examples include Oprah Winfrey, Richard Branson, and Jeff Bezos, who leverage their networks for growth and innovation.

6. Innovation and Adaptability:

Embracing innovation and remaining adaptable is essential. Leaders like Jeff Bezos with Amazon and Elon Musk with Tesla and SpaceX continuously push boundaries and adapt to new trends.

7. Long-Term Vision:

Focus on sustainable growth, long-lasting impact, and strategic planning over short-term gains. Leaders like Mark Zuckerberg, Larry Page, Sergey Brin, and Elon Musk invest in future technologies and innovations for lasting relevance and societal advancement.

These key points emphasize the importance of a proactive, strategic, and innovative approach to wealth accumulation and impact, illustrating how billionaires think and operate to achieve and sustain their success.

Chapter 3

Insightful Living: Breaking Free from Mental Blindness

"The greatest disability humanity suffers from is not physical but mental disabilities. The greatest blindness mankind suffers from is not eyesight but insight. A lack of vision leads to indecision, living a life without precision, devoid of definiteness of purpose."

C R Wallace.

Let's explore how the experiences of Stevie Wonder, Philip Danforth Armour Sr, Haben Girma, Helen Keller, and Nick Vujicic exemplify the theme of "Insightful Living: Breaking Free from Mental Blindness."

Stevie Wonder:

Despite being blind from infancy due to retinopathy of prematurity, Stevie Wonder became one of the most influential musicians of all time. His ability to perceive and interpret music goes beyond physical sight, showcasing how inner vision can overcome physical limitations. Wonder's extraordinary musical talent was evident from a young age; he was signed to Motown's Tamla label at just 11 years old, and by the age of 13, he had his first major hit with "Fingertips, Pt. 2."

Throughout his career, Wonder has continually pushed the boundaries of music with his innovative use of synthesizers and electronic instruments, blending genres such as soul, pop, jazz, and funk. Albums like "Innervisions," "Songs in the Key of Life," and "Talking Book" are considered masterpieces, reflecting his deep understanding of complex musical structures and profound lyrical content. His song "Superstition" is not only a classic hit but also a hallmark of his ability to infuse deep grooves with sophisticated rhythms.

Beyond his musical talents, Wonder's philanthropic contributions to society are profound. He has actively supported numerous charitable causes, advocating for social justice, equality, and accessibility for people with disabilities. In the 1980s, Wonder was a driving force behind the campaign to establish Martin Luther King Jr.'s birthday as a national holiday, using his platform to influence political change. His song "Happy Birthday" became an anthem for the movement.

His foundation, the Stevie Wonder House Full of Toys Benefit Concert, has raised millions of dollars to provide resources and support to children and families in need during the holiday season. This annual event exemplifies his commitment to giving back to the community and using his influence for positive change. Additionally, Wonder has been a UN Messenger of Peace with a special focus on persons with disabilities, amplifying his advocacy on a global stage.

Wonder's journey to musical greatness encountered financial hurdles early in his career, including disputes over royalties and the challenges of navigating the music industry as a young artist. Despite these obstacles, his resilience and creative vision illuminated paths of inspiration, showcasing how inner strength can overcome any obstacle. His life story is not just one of musical genius, but also of unwavering determination and a commitment to using his talents for the betterment of humanity.

Philip Danforth Armour Sr:

As the founder of Armour and Company, a meatpacking company, Armour faced numerous challenges in the business world. Despite his physical abilities, his vision and insight propelled him to success. His journey wasn't just about meat; it was a testament to the power of entrepreneurial spirit and innovation.

Armour revolutionized the meatpacking industry not only through innovative practices but also through strategic vision and adaptability. He foresaw market trends, embraced technological advancements, and implemented efficient processes, setting new standards for the industry. One of his key innovations was the introduction of refrigerated railroad cars in the 1870s, which transformed the distribution of perishable goods and allowed for the expansion of his market far beyond local boundaries. This innovation not only increased the shelf life of products but also enabled the nationwide distribution of fresh meat, significantly lowering costs and increasing accessibility.

Additionally, Armour's commitment to utilizing every part of the animal led to the development of by-products industries, such as the production of glue, soap, and fertilizers from previously discarded materials. This approach minimizes waste and maximizes profitability, showcasing his ability to think holistically about business operations.

Armour was also a pioneer in workforce management. He introduced a profit-sharing plan for his employees, which was quite progressive for its time. This not only improved worker morale and loyalty but also boosted productivity, creating a more motivated and efficient workforce. His forward-thinking approach to employee relations and corporate responsibility set a precedent for future business leaders.

His story illustrates that success isn't merely about physical prowess; it's about mental clarity, foresight, and the willingness to evolve. Armour's legacy continues to inspire generations, showing how perseverance and ingenuity can transform obstacles into stepping stones towards greatness. His impact on the meatpacking industry and business practices, in general, is a powerful reminder that true innovation lies in the ability to see beyond the present and adapt to the future.

Haben Girma: As the first deafblind graduate of Harvard Law School, Haben Girma's life story epitomizes the triumph of the human spirit over adversity. Despite facing significant challenges due to her disabilities, Girma refused to let them define her. Through her advocacy work, she has broken down barriers and championed disability rights, showcasing the importance of inner vision and determination in creating positive change.

Girma was born in Oakland, California, to Eritrean and Ethiopian parents, and her unique cultural background has played a significant role in shaping her perspectives and advocacy. Her journey to Harvard Law was marked by resilience and innovation. For instance, Girma developed a system for communicating in class by using a digital Braille device that allowed her to read and type responses in real-time, bridging the gap between her and her peers.

Her accomplishments extend far beyond her academic achievements. As an attorney, author, and public speaker, Girma has dedicated her career to advancing the rights of people with disabilities. She has worked with numerous organizations to promote accessibility in technology, education, and employment. One of her notable contributions includes consulting with tech companies like Apple to improve accessibility features, ensuring that digital tools are usable by all individuals, regardless of their physical abilities.

In her book, "Haben: The Deafblind Woman Who Conquered Harvard Law," Girma shares her personal experiences and insights, offering an inspiring narrative of perseverance and empowerment. Her story highlights the systemic barriers faced by people with disabilities and the importance of creating inclusive environments.

Girma's advocacy has earned her numerous accolades, including being named a White House Champion of Change by President Obama in 2013 and receiving the Helen Keller Achievement Award. Her impact is global, as she continues to travel and speak about the importance of accessibility and inclusion, inspiring countless individuals to challenge their limitations and advocate for equal rights.

Through her work, Haben Girma exemplifies how inner strength, innovation, and determination can transform personal challenges into catalysts for societal change. Her legacy is a powerful reminder that accessibility and inclusion are not just ideals but essential components of a just and equitable society.

elHelen Keller:

Born in 1880, Helen Keller was left deaf and blind at 19 months due to an illness, likely scarlet fever or meningitis. Despite these immense challenges, Keller overcame significant obstacles to become a renowned author, lecturer, and advocate for people with disabilities. Her early years were marked by frustration and isolation, unable to communicate effectively with those around her. This changed dramatically when Anne Sullivan, her dedicated teacher, entered her life in 1887.

Sullivan taught Keller to communicate using the manual alphabet, spelling words in her hand. This breakthrough moment, symbolized by the famous scene at the water pump where Keller first connected the sensation of water with the spelled-out word, unlocked her ability to connect with the world around her. Keller's relentless curiosity and Sullivan's innovative teaching methods led to her mastery of multiple languages, including French, German, Greek, and Latin. She achieved academic success, graduating cum laude from Radcliffe College in 1904, becoming the first deaf-blind person to earn a Bachelor of Arts degree.

Keller's determination to learn and communicate allowed her to break free from the mental blindness imposed by her disabilities, inspiring millions worldwide. She authored several books, including her autobiography "The Story of My Life," which details her early experiences and the transformative impact of education and perseverance. Keller's other notable works include "The World I Live In," "Out of the Dark," and "My Religion," each offering deep insights into her perceptions and thoughts.

Beyond her literary contributions, Keller was an outspoken advocate for disability rights, women's suffrage, and social equality. She used her platform to fight for justice and accessibility for all, working with organizations such as the American Foundation for the Blind and the American Civil Liberties Union. Keller's activism extended to international issues; she was a vocal supporter of pacifism and socialism, and she worked tirelessly to improve conditions for the blind worldwide.

Her legacy is a testament to the power of resilience and education. Keller's life story has been adapted into numerous plays and films, most famously the play and film "The Miracle Worker," which dramatizes the relationship between Keller and Sullivan. Helen Keller remains an enduring symbol of courage, intellect, and the indomitable human spirit.

Nick Vujicic:

Born in 1982 in Melbourne, Australia, without arms and legs due to a rare condition called tetra-amelia syndrome, Nick Vujicic faced significant challenges from a young age. He endured bullying and discrimination, which led to feelings of loneliness and despair during his childhood. Despite these physical and emotional struggles, Vujicic refused to let his disabilities define him. His journey from adversity to empowerment is a testament to the power of resilience and positive thinking.

Vujicic's transformation began when he realized that his worth was not determined by his physical limitations. Embracing his differences, he developed a strong sense of self and a passion for inspiring others. He began giving motivational talks at the age of 19, sharing his experiences and insights with audiences worldwide. His compelling message of hope, resilience, and inner strength has reached millions, demonstrating how mental barriers can be overcome through a positive mindset and unwavering determination.

His journey has taken him to over 70 countries, where he has addressed diverse audiences, including students, business professionals, and prisoners. Vujicic's dynamic speaking style and heartfelt story resonate deeply, encouraging others to overcome their own challenges and pursue a fulfilling and purposeful life. His outreach work extends beyond speaking engagements; he founded the non-profit organization Life Without Limbs, which provides support and resources to individuals facing physical and emotional obstacles. Through this organization, Vujicic advocates for the rights and inclusion of people with disabilities, offering practical help and hope.

Vujicic is also an accomplished author. His books, including "Life Without Limits," "Unstoppable," "Stand Strong," and "Love Without Limits," offer practical advice, personal anecdotes, and spiritual insights. These works underscore his belief that a life of purpose and joy is possible, regardless of physical limitations. He emphasizes themes of self-acceptance, faith, and the importance of a supportive community.

In addition to his writing and speaking, Vujicic has made appearances in various media outlets, sharing his message on television shows, podcasts, and online platforms. He is also known for his involvement in various humanitarian efforts, using his platform to address issues such as bullying, mental health, and the stigma surrounding disabilities.

Nick Vujicic's life story is a powerful example of overcoming adversity through inner strength and a positive outlook. His unwavering faith, dedication to helping others, and ability to inspire and motivate have made him a global symbol of resilience and hope. His work continues to impact countless lives, proving that with the right mindset, any challenge can be turned into an opportunity for growth and contribution.

These examples of courage and resilience illustrate how individuals can overcome physical and mental barriers to achieve extraordinary feats by embracing their inner vision, purpose, and resilience. Through their lives, Helen Keller, Nick Vujicic, Stevie Wonder, Philip Danforth Armour Sr., and Haben Girma inspire us to break free from limiting beliefs and strive for greatness despite any obstacles we may face. Their stories show that adversity can be transformed into opportunities for growth and development.

Helen Keller, born deaf and blind, exemplifies how determination and innovative teaching can break through seemingly insurmountable barriers. With the help of her teacher, Anne Sullivan, Keller learned to communicate and connect with the world, ultimately achieving academic success and becoming a prolific author and advocate for social justice. Her journey from isolation to intellectual and social prominence demonstrates the power of perseverance and the transformative impact of education.

Nick Vujicic, born without arms and legs, faced significant physical and emotional challenges but refused to let his disabilities define him. Through motivational speaking and his non-profit organization, Life Without Limbs, Vujicic spreads a message of hope and resilience. His ability to inspire millions worldwide with his story and practical advice underscores the potential for inner strength and a positive mindset to overcome any challenge.

Stevie Wonder, blind from birth, became one of the most successful and influential musicians of all time. His exceptional talent, combined with an unwavering commitment to his craft, allowed him to transcend his disability and produce timeless music that has touched the hearts of millions. Wonder's achievements highlight the importance of passion and perseverance in achieving greatness.

Philip Danforth Armour Sr., an influential American industrialist and philanthropist, overcame early financial struggles to build one of the largest meatpacking firms in the world. His innovative approaches to business and commitment to improving conditions for his workers exemplify how vision and resilience can lead to monumental success. Armour's legacy includes significant contributions to education and social welfare, reflecting his dedication to using his achievements for the greater good.

Haben Girma:

The first deaf-blind graduate of Harvard Law School, is a leading advocate for disability rights and accessibility. Her work has paved the way for greater inclusivity and equal opportunities for people with disabilities. Girma's achievements underscore the impact of education and advocacy in breaking down barriers and creating a more inclusive society.

These individuals teach us that our limitations do not determine our potential. By embracing their inner vision and purpose, they have not only overcome their disabilities but have also contributed significantly to society. Their lives are powerful reminders that obstacles can be turned into opportunities for personal growth and development, inspiring us all to pursue our dreams with determination and courage.

Summary:

The chapter "Insightful Living: Breaking Free from Mental Blindness" emphasizes that the greatest disabilities are not physical but mental, with a lack of vision leading to indecision and a life without purpose. This theme is exemplified through the lives of Stevie Wonder, Philip Danforth Armour Sr., Haben Girma, Helen Keller, and Nick Vujicic. Each of these individuals has overcome significant challenges to achieve extraordinary feats by embracing their inner vision, purpose, and resilience. Their stories inspire us to break free from limiting beliefs and transform obstacles into opportunities for growth and development.

Key Takeaways

1. Mental Disabilities vs. Physical Disabilities:

The most significant disabilities are mental, not physical. A lack of vision and insight can lead to a life without direction or purpose.

2. Stevie Wonder:

Despite being blind from infancy, Stevie Wonder became a legendary musician. His inner vision and talent allowed him to transcend physical limitations and innovate in music. Wonder's philanthropy and advocacy for social justice highlight his commitment to using his influence for positive change.

3. Philip Danforth Armour Sr.:

Armour revolutionized the meatpacking industry with innovative practices and strategic vision. His entrepreneurial spirit and commitment to employee welfare set new standards in business. Armour's legacy demonstrates that success stems from mental clarity, foresight, and adaptability.

4. Haben Girma:

As the first deaf-blind graduate of Harvard Law School, Girma is a leading advocate for disability rights. Her innovations in communication and advocacy work have significantly advanced accessibility. Girma's achievements underscore the importance of creating inclusive environments and breaking down barriers.

5. Helen Keller:

Born deaf and blind, Keller overcame immense obstacles to become a renowned author and advocate. Her determination and innovative teaching methods led to academic and social success. Keller's advocacy for disability rights and social equality demonstrates the transformative power of education and resilience.

6. Nick Vujicic:

Born without arms and legs, Vujicic faced significant physical and emotional challenges. His motivational speaking and non-profit organization, Life Without Limbs, inspires millions worldwide. Vujicic's life story is a testament to the power of inner strength and a positive mindset in overcoming challenges.

7. Transformation of Adversity:

The stories of these individuals illustrate that limitations do not determine potential. Embracing inner vision and purpose can turn obstacles into opportunities for growth and development. Their lives are powerful reminders to pursue dreams with determination and courage, regardless of physical or mental barriers.

These examples teach us that with vision, purpose, and resilience, anyone can overcome mental and physical barriers to achieve greatness and inspire others.

Chapter 4
Finding Truth in Contradiction

"Embracing 'Good Guys Come Last' "There are many sayings I disagree with. However, through life experiences, I have learned to accept this truth: 'Good guys come last.' I had problems with that saying for a while because I consider myself a 'Good Guy.' Now, I believe this saying 100 percent. I encourage you, men, to stop being a good guy and become a great man."

C R Wallace

The Transformation of Clarence Wallace:

I once went to a detention center to teach a class. The room that I was using to facilitate the class was at the front of the institution, and the room had large glass windows that added lighting to the room.

However, throughout the day, I saw the most beautiful women ever in one single day, entering and leaving the building. After a while, I could not resist asking the participants in the class, "Why are so many beautiful women going in and out of the building?" I was amazed at the response I got. One of the participants said to me they are girlfriends and wives of the inmates, and many of them have multiple women who sometimes fight over them.

I am by no means advising any man to be bad and do bad things to become an inmate in a prison institution. However, this experience gave me something to ponder as a professional student who is open to learning more about different aspects of life. I decided to do some research into this matter which led me to revisit the saying "Good guys come last." I am now fully convinced that the saying "Good guys come last." is truth. As I mentioned earlier, I don't endorse being a bad guy. However, let's examine this saying.

I found the saying "Good guys come last" to be true regardless of the setting, be it personal, casual, or professional relationships. Let me expound on what the saying "Good guys come last" means. A good guy is a guy who makes others happy at their expense, a guy who over apologizes even when they are right to keep the peace, one who is loyal to people who are disloyal to them, cares more about the feelings of others than their own, and shows kindness to people who are unkind to them. This is not an exhaustive list; I could go on and on. However, I believe you get the point.

I was once a good-hearted individual who often found myself being taken advantage of in different situations due to my kindness. Many people misinterpreted my kindness as weakness or as a desire for their approval. Here are some examples of my experiences in the role of the 'good guy': In religious settings, I encountered leaders and individuals who attempted to exploit their positions of influence and authority to manipulate me into conforming to their wishes.

In professional environments, I faced individuals who used flattery to try to control me, attempting to influence me to compromise my principles and integrity in order to align with their own ideologies.

On a personal level, I have encountered various family members and friends who tried to impose their expectations on me and define who they believed I should be. At times, they even disregarded the boundaries of our relationship to influence my decisions about my future.

I have always respected the autonomy of my adult children. It's disheartening to experience such disrespect from these individuals.

In the various aspects of the relationships I mentioned, these individuals often behaved as if they were demigods in my life.

Allow me to clarify: I was never a pushover. However, there were many occasions when I chose to overlook things in order to maintain peace. Looking back, I realize how foolish that was. It's akin to someone ignoring aggressive cancerous cells in their body.

The Transformation Begins:

Like a caterpillar transforming into a butterfly, we must die to our old identity to experience freedom from mediocrity to fulfill our destiny, rising to become pollinators, influencers who positively uplift the lives of others in our sphere of influence. No longer confined to crawling on the ground, but soaring freely beyond the judgments of men. With this understanding, I realize I don't require the validation of others to fulfill my purpose; with God as my ally, I am already in the majority.

When God is on your side, victory is assured. The battle belongs to the Lord, and triumph is yours.

Embracing Greatness:

I am no longer just a good guy; I strive to be a great man, dedicated to fulfilling my purpose of positively influencing the lives of others to make a lasting impact on many. The transformation has brought a profound liberty into my life. As the scriptures declare, "Whom the Son made free is free indeed." I am no longer shackled by the opinions of others; they hold no place in my mind. They have been evicted permanently, buried and forgotten, leaving no trace behind, vanished into eternity. It feels incredible to be liberated.

Transformation symbolizes not just a personal change. It represents a universal truth that we all have the potential to rise above the limitations imposed by others and our own past selves. By shedding the "good guy" persona that often leads to exploitation and stepping into a role of strength and purpose, we can achieve true greatness and make a positive, lasting impact on the world. This journey is about embracing who we are meant to be and living a life that is true to our values and calling, free from the constraints of seeking external approval.

I found the saying "Good guys come last" to be true regardless of the setting, be it personal, casual, or professional relationships. Let me expound on what the saying "Good guys come last" means. A good guy is a guy who makes others happy at their expense, a guy who over apologizes even when they are right to keep the peace, one who is loyal to people who are disloyal to them, cares more about the feelings of others than their own, and shows kindness to people who are unkind to them. This is not an exhaustive list; I could go on and on. However, I would often find myself being taken advantage of in different situations due to my kindness. Many people misinterpreted my kindness as a sign of weakness or as a desire for their approval. Here are some examples of my experiences in the role of the 'good guy':

In religious settings, I encountered leaders and individuals who attempted to exploit their positions of influence and authority to manipulate me into conforming to their wishes.

In professional environments, I faced individuals who used

flattery to try to control me, attempting to influence me to compromise my principles and integrity in order to align with their own ideologies.

On a personal level, I have encountered various family members and friends who tried to impose their expectations on me and define who they believed I should be. At times, they even disregarded the boundaries of our relationship to influence my decisions about my future.

I have always respected the autonomy of my adult children. It's disheartening to experience such disrespect from these individuals.

In the various aspects of the relationships I mentioned, these individuals often behaved as if they were demigods in my life.

Allow me to clarify: I was never a pushover. However, there were many occasions when I chose to overlook things in order to maintain peace. Looking back, I realize how foolish that was. It's akin to someone ignoring aggressive cancerous cells in their body.

Like a caterpillar transformation into a butterfly, so we must die to our old identity to experience freedom from mediocrity to fulfill our destiny, rising to become pollinators, influencers to positively uplifting the lives of others in our sphere of influence.

No longer confined to mediocrity, but soaring freely beyond

the judgments of men. With this understanding, I realize I don't require the validation of others to fulfill my purpose; with God as my ally, I am already in the majority.

When God is on your side, victory is assured. The battle belongs to the Lord, and triumph is yours.

I am no longer just a good guy; I strive to be a great man, dedicated to fulfilling my purpose of positively influencing the lives of others to make a lasting impact on many.

I am experiencing a profound liberty, as the scriptures declare, 'Whom the Son makes free is free indeed.' I am no longer shackled by the opinions of others; they hold no place in my mind. They have been evicted permanently, buried and forgotten, leaving no trace behind, vanished into eternity. It feels incredible to be liberated.

I pray that readers or listeners of this book will be liberated from the snares, traps, and nets set by others to hinder them from fulfilling their destiny. Proverbs 20:25 states, 'The fear of man brings a snare: but whoever trusts in the Lord shall be safe.'

True liberation involves being free from the opinions of others. Throughout history, many courageous men and women have faced imprisonment or even death for standing firm in their convictions, from figures in the Old and New Testaments to modern icons like Nelson Mandela, and countless individuals, including law enforcement officers who dedicate themselves to serving and protecting our communities.

I deliberately use 'died' instead of 'losing their lives' because no one can extinguish the true spirit of a person; they can only affect the 'earth suit,' the physical body that houses our purpose in life. As Matthew 10:28 states, 'And do not fear those who kill the body but cannot kill the soul. Rather, fear him, who can destroy both soul and body in hell.

What I learned from the prison guards regarding the prisoners who received regular visits from these beautiful women, offering them more attention than many free men, is that living authentically earns respect and admiration, even when engaging in wrongdoing. Individuals of courage are admired for their authenticity, rather than imitation. As mentioned earlier, I do not condone violence or illegal activities.

This is akin to eating fish and discarding the bones; in life, even fools can offer lessons. Sometimes, the lesson is simply learning what not to do, a truth in itself. The lesson learned from the prison guards regarding the prisoners is that a person can be physically imprisoned yet mentally liberated, while seemingly free members of society can be physically free but mentally bound. True freedom is not based on where one resides, but on the liberation of the mind.

I believe the greatest freedom is the freedom of speech and expression. Unfortunately, many are imprisoned by those who seek control and power, at the expense of kind-hearted souls. It's important to note that freedom should never be used to harm others; instead, it should be used to liberate and uplift them.

I conclude by saying this: stop being a good guy and become a great man by being authentic in a world that's filled with fake people. You will stand out with no effort. Being real is the greatest challenge most people face because they are afraid of being judged by others. I would encourage you that if people have time to judge you and watch you, they are in the peanut gallery. You are a star.

Stop striving to be a good guy and aim to become a great man by embracing authenticity in a world filled with superficiality. Authenticity effortlessly sets you apart. Many people struggle with being genuine because they fear judgment from others. I urge you, if people have the time to judge and watch you, they're in the peanut gallery—you're the star. So, shine brightly like a guiding star, illuminating the darkness of the world.

Embracing the truth that 'good guys come last' has been a transformative journey for me. Through life's trials, I've learned that prioritizing others' needs often resulted in exploitation. However, this realization isn't about advocating for negativity, but rather about asserting oneself authentically.

By shedding the 'good guy' persona, I've embraced greatness, standing firm in my principles, positively influencing others, and living authentically without seeking validation. This transition liberated me from others' opinions, allowing me to pursue my purpose boldly.

Key Points from the Chapter:

1. The author initially struggled with the saying "Good guys come last" but eventually came to embrace it through life experiences.

2. An encounter at a detention center prompted the author to reflect on the truth behind the saying.

3. The author defines what it means to be a "good guy," highlighting behaviors such as prioritizing others' happiness over one's own and being overly accommodating.

4. Personal anecdotes illustrate how the author was taken advantage of due to his kindness and accommodating nature.

5. The author decides to let go of the "good guy" persona and embrace being a "great man," emphasizing authenticity and

self-assertion.

6. A metaphor of transformation from a caterpillar to a butterfly symbolizes the author's journey of self-discovery and liberation.

7. The author finds freedom in being true to oneself, unaffected by the opinions of others.

8. A call to action urges readers to break free from societal expectations and embrace authenticity, shining brightly in a world filled with darkness.

9. The importance of using freedom to uplift and liberate others is emphasized over using it to harm.

10. The conclusion encapsulates the transformative journey of embracing the truth behind the saying and encourages others to do the same.

Chapter 5

Behavior Shapes Brand Identity
Hypocrisy's Toll: Brand Implosion Unveiled

"Behavior is the brand! Not belief! Behavior that is not in alignment with belief is hypocrisy and will cause an organization, business, and even a family to implode."

Clarence R. Wallace.

In the realm of branding, behavior reigns supreme. Actions speak louder than beliefs, and behavior that contradicts beliefs breeds hypocrisy, leading to the downfall of organizations, businesses, and families alike. When a company's actions do not align with its stated values and promises, it risks losing the trust and loyalty of its customers. For instance, a brand that champions sustainability but engages in environmentally harmful practices will be viewed as hypocritical, undermining its credibility and damaging its reputation.

This principle applies equally to individuals and families. Parents who preach honesty but are frequently caught in lies set a poor example for their children, fostering an environment of mistrust. Similarly, leaders who advocate for ethical behavior but engage in corruption erode their followers' confidence. In both personal and professional contexts, consistent and authentic behavior is crucial for building and maintaining trust. Organizations that align their actions with their stated values are more likely to cultivate a loyal customer base, retain talented employees, and enjoy long-term success. Conversely, those that fail to do so may experience significant fallout, including public backlash, loss of revenue, and diminished morale among employees.

When it comes to brand identity, behavior is paramount. A brand's actions must align seamlessly with its stated beliefs and values to maintain credibility. This alignment builds trust, a fundamental component of any successful relationship, whether it be between a company and its customers, an organization and its members, or within a family. When there is a disconnect between what a brand claims to stand for and how it actually behaves, it creates a sense of hypocrisy. This perceived hypocrisy can be incredibly damaging, as it not only erodes trust but also undermines the very foundation upon which the entity is built. For businesses, this can lead to a loss of customer loyalty, negative publicity, and, ultimately, financial decline. In organizations, such inconsistencies can result in decreased employee morale, disengagement, and high turnover rates. Within families, misalignment between beliefs and actions can cause emotional rifts and breakdowns in communication. Therefore, ensuring consistency between declared values and real-world actions is critical for the sustainability and integrity of any entity.

A strong brand identity hinges on consistent behavior. It's not enough for an organization, business, or family to merely profess certain beliefs and values; these principles must be reflected in everyday actions and decisions. When actions deviate from professed beliefs, they sow the seeds of hypocrisy, creating a discord that can be deeply damaging. This inconsistency threatens the integrity and cohesion of any group, eroding trust and credibility.

For organizations, this means that leadership must not only articulate a clear vision and set of values but also demonstrate these through policies, culture, and everyday interactions. Employees look to leaders as role models, and any perceived hypocrisy can lead to disengagement, lower morale, and a toxic work environment.

In the business context, customers are increasingly savvy and values-driven. They scrutinize whether a company's actions align with its marketing messages. If a business claims to prioritize sustainability but engages in environmentally harmful practices, for example, it risks backlash, boycotts, and a damaged reputation, which can be difficult to recover from.

Within families, the principle of aligning actions with beliefs is equally critical. Parents and guardians serve as the primary role models for their children. When there is a gap between what parents say and what they do, children may become confused and distrustful. This can lead to strained relationships and a breakdown in family communication. Over time, these issues can create lasting emotional and psychological impacts, potentially fracturing the family unit.

Ultimately, consistent behavior that aligns with stated beliefs is essential for maintaining trust, integrity, and cohesion. This alignment fosters a stable and reliable identity that others can believe in and support, ensuring the long-term success and health of organizations, businesses, and families.

In branding, behavior is the cornerstone upon which trust is built. Trust, being a fragile yet vital element, requires that an organization's actions consistently reflect its stated beliefs and values. When there is a misalignment between belief and action, it breeds hypocrisy. This perceived hypocrisy doesn't just cause minor damage; it fundamentally corrodes the very foundations upon which organizations, businesses, and families are built.

For organizations, such as non-profits or companies, the damage from hypocrisy can be severe. Stakeholders, including employees, investors, and customers, expect congruence between an entity's mission statement and its daily operations. When a company promotes itself as a champion of ethical practices but fails to uphold these in its supply chain or labor policies, it risks losing stakeholder trust. This loss of trust can lead to reduced employee engagement, customer boycotts, and a decline in investor confidence, ultimately threatening the organization's viability.

Businesses, in particular, face the constant scrutiny of a socially aware and connected consumer base. Modern consumers not only purchase products but also buy into the values and ethics of the brands they support. A business that espouses environmental consciousness yet engages in pollution or unsustainable practices will quickly find itself at the center of public criticism. Social media amplifies such discrepancies, potentially leading to widespread reputational damage and a sharp decline in customer loyalty.

Therefore, ensuring that behavior aligns with proclaimed beliefs is not just a matter of maintaining a good image; it is essential for preserving the integrity, trust, and cohesion that underpin successful and resilient organizations, businesses, and families. Consistent, value-driven behavior fosters a stable foundation that can withstand challenges and support sustained growth and harmony.

Behavior serves as the litmus test for brand integrity. It is through consistent actions that a brand, organization, business, or family proves its commitment to its stated beliefs and values. When behavior aligns with these professed principles, it reinforces trust and reliability. However, misalignment between belief and action is a recipe for hypocrisy. This hypocrisy poses a grave threat to the stability and sustainability of any entity, ultimately resulting in its collapse.

For organizations, integrity is crucial. Stakeholders, including employees, clients, and partners, expect that the organization's actions reflect its core values. For instance, a company that touts its dedication to diversity and inclusion must actively implement policies and practices that support this commitment. Any deviation, such as discriminatory hiring practices or a non-inclusive workplace culture, can lead to a loss of trust and credibility. Employees may feel disillusioned and disengaged, which can result in high turnover rates and a toxic work environment. Clients and partners may choose to distance themselves, leading to financial and reputational damage.

In the business world, integrity is equally important. Today's consumers are highly informed and have access to a wealth of information about corporate practices. They are quick to hold businesses accountable for any discrepancies between their stated values and their actions. A business that claims to prioritize customer satisfaction but delivers poor customer service, or one that markets itself as environmentally conscious while engaging in unsustainable practices, will likely face public backlash. This can manifest in negative reviews, social media outrage, and even organized boycotts, all of which can severely impact the business's bottom line and long-term viability.

Families also rely on the alignment of actions and beliefs to maintain trust and cohesion. Parents and guardians are often seen as the moral and ethical guides for their children. When there is a disconnect between what parents say and what they do, children may become confused and distrustful. This can lead to strained relationships and a breakdown in family communication. Over time, these issues can create lasting emotional and psychological impacts, potentially fracturing the family unit.

Examples of Companies: Succeeded with Aligned Behavior:

Patagonia: Commitment to Environmental Sustainability

Overview:

Patagonia, a leading outdoor apparel brand, is celebrated for its unwavering commitment to environmental sustainability. Founded in 1973 by Yvon Chouinard, Patagonia has built a strong reputation for aligning its business operations with its environmental values. This alignment is evident in every aspect of the company's operations, from product design and material sourcing to corporate activism and community engagement.

Eco-friendly Practices:

Patagonia integrates sustainable practices across its supply chain. The company prioritizes the use of organic cotton, recycled polyester, and other environmentally friendly materials. Patagonia's dedication to quality ensures that its products are durable, reducing the need for frequent replacements and minimizing environmental impact. The company's production processes are designed to minimize waste and energy consumption, reflecting its commitment to reducing its ecological footprint.

Worn Wear Program:

One of Patagonia's standout initiatives is the "Worn Wear" program, which encourages customers to repair, reuse, and recycle their clothing. This program promotes a culture of sustainability by extending the life cycle of products and reducing waste. Patagonia offers repair services for its products, and through Worn Wear, customers can trade in used items for store credit, which are then cleaned and resold. This initiative not only supports environmental goals but also reinforces the brand's commitment to reducing the environmental impact of fast fashion.

Corporate Activism:

Patagonia actively participates in environmental activism and advocacy. The company donates 1% of its sales to environmental causes through its "1% for the Planet" program, contributing millions of dollars annually to grassroots environmental organizations. Patagonia also engages in political activism, supporting policies and candidates that advocate for environmental protection. The company's leadership, including founder Yvon Chouinard, has been vocal about the urgent need for corporate responsibility in addressing climate change and environmental degradation.

Innovative Initiatives:

Patagonia continually seeks innovative ways to enhance its sustainability efforts. The company has invested in regenerative organic agriculture, which aims to restore soil health and sequester carbon, thereby mitigating climate change. Patagonia also launched the "Action Works" platform, connecting individuals with local environmental groups and initiatives, further empowering its community to engage in environmental activism.

Impact and Customer Loyalty:

Patagonia's consistent and authentic commitment to environmental sustainability has cultivated a loyal customer base. Consumers who prioritize sustainability and ethical practices are drawn to Patagonia, not just for its high-quality products but also for its principled stance on environmental issues. The brand's transparency about its efforts and challenges in sustainability fosters trust and strengthens its reputation as a leader in corporate responsibility.

Conclusion:

Patagonia exemplifies how aligning business operations

with core environmental values can lead to a successful and respected brand. By integrating sustainable practices into every facet of its operations and actively participating in environmental advocacy, Patagonia has built a loyal customer base and set a benchmark for corporate responsibility. The company's ongoing efforts to innovate and lead in sustainability demonstrate that a genuine commitment to environmental values can drive both business success and positive change.

Examples of Companies:

Ben & Jerry's: Championing Social Responsibility and Activism

Overview:

Ben & Jerry's, a beloved ice cream company founded in 1978 by Ben Cohen and Jerry Greenfield, has become synonymous with social responsibility and activism. From its inception, Ben & Jerry's has prioritized values-driven business practices, integrating social and environmental concerns into its mission and operations.

Emphasis on Social Justice:

Ben & Jerry's is renowned for its vocal advocacy on various social justice issues, including racial equality, and climate change. The company uses its platform to amplify marginalized voices and advocate for systemic change. Through campaigns, partnerships, and public statements, Ben & Jerry's actively engages in dialogue and action around pressing social issues, demonstrating its commitment to driving positive change beyond profit.

Ethical Sourcing Practices:

Central to Ben & Jerry's commitment to social responsibility is its sourcing of Fairtrade-certified ingredients. By partnering with Fairtrade-certified suppliers, the company ensures that farmers and workers receive fair wages and operate under safe and humane working conditions. This commitment extends to supporting sustainable agriculture practices, such as organic farming, which promote environmental stewardship and biodiversity conservation.

Founder Advocacy:

Ben Cohen and Jerry Greenfield, the company's founders, have been instrumental in using their platform to advocate for progressive causes. Both founders are outspoken activists who leverage their influence and resources to champion social justice initiatives. From participating in protests to lobbying for policy changes, Ben & Jerry's founders exemplify the brand's ethos of using business as a force for good. Their personal commitment to activism reinforces the brand's integrity and authenticity, resonating with consumers who share similar values.

Community Engagement:

Ben & Jerry's actively engages with communities through philanthropic initiatives and grassroots activism. The company supports local organizations and initiatives that align with its values, contributing to community development and empowerment. Through events, partnerships, and volunteerism, Ben & Jerry's fosters connections with its customers and communities, creating a sense of belonging and shared purpose.

Impact and Consumer Loyalty:

Ben & Jerry's unwavering commitment to social responsibility and activism has earned it a loyal following of consumers who value ethical business practices and social justice advocacy. By aligning its values with its actions, Ben & Jerry's has built trust and credibility among consumers, who view the brand as a genuine advocate for positive change. This consumer loyalty translates into continued support for the brand and its products, reinforcing the business case for corporate social responsibility.

Conclusion:

Ben & Jerry's exemplifies how a company can integrate social responsibility and activism into its core business model, driving both positive social impact and business success. Through its emphasis on social justice, ethical sourcing practices, founder advocacy, and community engagement, Ben & Jerry's has established itself as a leader in values-driven business. The brand's authenticity and integrity resonate with consumers, fostering loyalty and trust that extends beyond mere transactions. Ben & Jerry's serves as a compelling example of how businesses can use their influence and resources to effect meaningful change in society while remaining profitable and sustainable.

TOMS: Driving Social Impact Through the "One for One" Model

Overview:

TOMS, founded in 2006 by Blake Mycoskie, has revolutionized the concept of corporate social responsibility with its innovative "One for One" model. This model, rooted in the ethos of giving back, has become synonymous with TOMS' brand identity and has had a transformative impact on communities around the world.

The "One for One" Model:

At the heart of TOMS' business model is the "One for One" concept, where every product sold results in a corresponding donation to someone in need. This model initially focused on shoes, with TOMS donating a pair of shoes to a child in need for every pair purchased. Over time, the "One for One" model has expanded to include other essential goods and services, such as eyewear, clean water, and safe birth services. Through these initiatives, TOMS aims to address various societal challenges, from poverty and preventable blindness to maternal and child health.

Transparent and Measurable Impact:

One of the key strengths of TOMS' approach to social impact is its transparency and measurability. The company is committed to providing customers with visibility into the tangible difference their purchases make in the lives of others. TOMS tracks and shares data on the number of shoes donated, eyewear distributed, and other metrics related to its social initiatives, allowing customers to see the direct impact of their support. This transparency enhances trust and reinforces the brand's credibility among socially conscious consumers.

Expanding Social Impact Initiatives:

In addition to its flagship shoe donation program, TOMS has diversified its social impact initiatives to address a broader range of needs. The company's "TOMS Eyewear" program provides prescription glasses, medical treatment, and sight-saving surgeries to individuals in underserved communities. TOMS also partners with organizations to provide access to clean water and safe birth services, furthering its commitment to improving health outcomes and quality of life for those in need. By continually expanding its social impact efforts, TOMS demonstrates a deepening commitment to creating positive change on a global scale.

Brand Identity and Consumer Appeal:

TOMS' "One for One" model has been instrumental in shaping its brand identity and resonating with socially conscious consumers. The company's commitment to social impact goes beyond mere corporate philanthropy; it is an integral part of TOMS' DNA and value proposition. By aligning its mission with its actions, TOMS has cultivated a strong, positive brand image that appeals to consumers who seek to make a meaningful difference through their purchases. The emotional connection formed through TOMS' social impact initiatives fosters customer loyalty and advocacy, driving continued support for the brand.

Conclusion:

TOMS exemplifies how a business can leverage its operations to drive positive social change and create a sustainable business model. Through its "One for One" model, TOMS has made a tangible difference in the lives of millions of people worldwide, addressing critical needs and fostering community development. By prioritizing transparency, measurability, and continuous innovation in its social impact initiatives, TOMS has built a brand that resonates deeply with socially conscious consumers. The success of TOMS serves as a testament to the power of business as a force for good and inspires other companies to embrace purpose-driven approaches to business.

Failed Due to Misalignment:

Wells Fargo: Wells Fargo's reputation as a trusted financial institution was severely damaged by a series of scandals involving deceptive practices. The most notable scandal involved employees creating millions of unauthorized accounts to meet sales targets. Despite Wells Fargo's public positioning as a customer-centric and ethical bank, these actions revealed a stark misalignment between its professed values and its internal practices. The fallout included significant financial penalties, a loss of customer trust, and a tarnished brand image that the company continues to struggle with.

Enron: Enron's collapse is one of the most infamous examples of corporate fraud. The energy company projected an image of success and innovation, but its internal reality was characterized by unethical accounting practices and extensive fraud. Enron's leadership manipulated financial statements to hide debt and inflate profits, misleading investors and employees. When the truth emerged, Enron declared bankruptcy, leading to massive financial losses, legal repercussions, and a complete loss of trust in the company.

Volkswagen: Volkswagen's reputation was severely damaged by the "Dieselgate" scandal, where the company was found to have installed software in its diesel vehicles to cheat emissions tests. Volkswagen had marketed these cars as environmentally friendly, aligning with a growing consumer preference for green technology. However, the revelation that the company had intentionally deceived regulators and customers about the environmental impact of its vehicles led to a significant loss of trust, massive financial penalties, and a damaged brand image that still affects the company today.

Conclusion:

These examples illustrate the profound impact that alignment or misalignment between professed values and actual behavior can have on a company's success and reputation. Companies like Patagonia, Ben & Jerry's, and TOMS have thrived by staying true to their core values and ensuring their actions consistently reflect their stated commitments. In contrast, companies like Wells Fargo, Enron, and Volkswagen have faced severe consequences due to the hypocrisy of their actions, which eroded trust and led to significant reputational and financial damage.

The lessons drawn from these case studies underscore the importance of authenticity, transparency, and ethical behavior in building and maintaining a strong brand. Organizations that prioritize aligning their actions with their values are more likely to earn and retain the trust and loyalty of their stakeholders, ensuring long-term success and resilience.

Failed Due to Misalignment:

Wells Fargo: Betrayal of Trust and Deceptive Practices

Overview:

Wells Fargo, one of the largest banks in the United States, experienced a dramatic downfall due to a series of scandals involving deceptive practices and ethical breaches. Despite its long-standing reputation as a trusted financial institution, Wells Fargo's misalignment between its professed values and internal practices led to severe consequences and a tarnished brand image.

Deceptive Sales Practices:

The most infamous scandal that rocked Wells Fargo involved employees creating millions of unauthorized accounts without customers' knowledge or consent. These accounts were opened to meet aggressive sales targets set by the bank, leading to widespread customer harm and unethical behavior within the organization. The revelation of these deceptive sales practices exposed a significant gap between Wells Fargo's outward image of customer-centricity and its internal culture of prioritizing sales over ethical conduct.

Misalignment with Stated Values:

Wells Fargo had long positioned itself as a customer-centric and ethical bank, emphasizing trust, integrity, and transparency in its communications and branding. However, the scandal exposed a stark misalignment between the company's professed values and its actual business practices. The egregious nature of the misconduct, coupled with the scale of the deception, eroded trust and credibility in Wells Fargo's brand, undermining its reputation as a reliable and ethical financial institution.

Consequences and Fallout:

The fallout from the Wells Fargo scandal was significant and far-reaching. The bank faced substantial financial penalties from regulatory authorities, including fines amounting to billions of dollars. In addition to the financial repercussions, Wells Fargo experienced a loss of customer trust and loyalty, as many customers felt betrayed and deceived by the bank's actions. The tarnished brand image and damaged reputation continue to haunt Wells Fargo, impacting its ability to attract new customers and retain existing ones.

Rebuilding Trust and Recovery Efforts:

In the aftermath of the scandal, Wells Fargo embarked on extensive efforts to rebuild trust and repair its damaged reputation. The bank implemented reforms and internal controls to prevent similar misconduct in the future, including changes to its incentive structures and corporate culture. However, rebuilding trust and restoring confidence in the brand remains an ongoing challenge for Wells Fargo, as the repercussions of the scandal continue to linger in the public consciousness.

Lessons Learned:

The Wells Fargo scandal serves as a cautionary tale about the importance of alignment between stated values and actual business practices. It underscores the devastating consequences that can arise when organizations prioritize short-term profits and sales targets over ethical conduct and customer trust. The scandal also highlights the critical role of transparency, accountability, and ethical leadership in maintaining the integrity of corporate brands and safeguarding stakeholder interests. Ultimately, the Wells Fargo case underscores the imperative for organizations to uphold ethical standards and ensure alignment between their actions and professed values to avoid reputational damage and loss of trust.

Enron: The Spectacular Collapse Amidst Ethical Failures

Overview:

Enron, once hailed as one of the most innovative and successful companies in the United States, ultimately met its demise in a spectacular fashion due to a web of unethical practices and financial fraud. The collapse of Enron sent shockwaves through the business world and led to significant regulatory reforms aimed at preventing similar corporate scandals in the future.

Rise to Prominence:

Enron's rise to prominence was fueled by its innovative business model and aggressive pursuit of growth opportunities in the energy sector. The company positioned itself as a pioneer in energy trading and market deregulation, leveraging complex financial instruments and creative accounting techniques to maximize profits and inflate its stock price. At its peak, Enron was regarded as a shining example of corporate success and was lauded for its seemingly unstoppable growth trajectory.

Ethical Breaches and Financial Fraud:

Behind the façade of success, Enron was engaged in a range of unethical practices and financial fraud schemes. The company used off-balance-sheet entities and special purpose vehicles to conceal debt and artificially inflate earnings, painting a misleading picture of its financial health to investors and analysts. Enron's executives, including CEO Jeffrey Skilling and CFO Andrew Fastow, orchestrated these schemes to enrich themselves and maintain the illusion of prosperity.

Collapse and Bankruptcy:

The House of Cards came crashing down in late 2001 when Enron's financial misdeeds were exposed, triggering a rapid and dramatic collapse. The company's stock price plummeted, wiping out billions of dollars in shareholder value virtually overnight. Enron filed for bankruptcy protection in December 2001, marking one of the largest corporate bankruptcies in U.S. history at the time. The fallout from Enron's collapse was far-reaching, leading to massive job losses, investor lawsuits, and regulatory investigations.

Impact on Stakeholders:

The collapse of Enron had devastating consequences for its stakeholders, including employees, shareholders, creditors, and the broader financial markets. Thousands of employees lost their jobs and retirement savings as Enron's stock became worthless virtually overnight. Shareholders saw their investments evaporate, while creditors faced substantial losses on loans and investments tied to the company. The shockwaves from Enron's collapse reverberated throughout the financial markets, undermining investor confidence and prompting calls for greater transparency and oversight in corporate governance.

Legacy and Lessons Learned:

The Enron scandal stands as a cautionary tale about the dangers of unchecked corporate greed, unethical behavior, and lax regulatory oversight. It exposed the flaws in Enron's corporate culture, characterized by a relentless pursuit of profit at any cost and a disregard for ethical principles and fiduciary responsibilities. The collapse of Enron led to sweeping reforms in corporate governance, accounting standards, and securities regulations, including the passage of the Sarbanes-Oxley Act in 2002, aimed at restoring investor confidence and enhancing transparency and accountability in financial reporting. Enron's legacy serves as a stark reminder of the importance of ethical leadership, transparency, and integrity in corporate governance and underscores the need for robust oversight mechanisms to prevent corporate misconduct and protect the interests of stakeholders.

Volkswagen: The Emissions Scandal and Betrayal of Trust

Overview:

Volkswagen, one of the world's largest automakers, faced a significant crisis when it was revealed that the company had engaged in widespread deception regarding its environmental responsibility. The scandal, known as the "Dieselgate" emissions scandal, tarnished Volkswagen's reputation and led to substantial financial and reputational damage.

Environmental Responsibility and Deception:

Volkswagen had long marketed itself as a leader in environmental responsibility, emphasizing its commitment to producing clean, fuel-efficient vehicles that minimize environmental impact. However, it was later discovered that Volkswagen had installed illegal software, known as "defeat devices," in millions of its diesel vehicles to cheat emissions tests. These defeat devices allowed the vehicles to pass regulatory emissions tests while emitting pollutants at levels far exceeding legal limits during real-world driving conditions. The revelation of this deception shattered the public's trust in Volkswagen and undermined the company's claims of environmental stewardship.

Impact on Consumers and the Environment:

The Volkswagen emissions scandal had far-reaching consequences for both consumers and the environment. Owners of affected Volkswagen vehicles felt betrayed and deceived by the company's actions, as they had purchased these vehicles under the belief that they were environmentally friendly. The emissions from these vehicles also contributed to air pollution and environmental degradation, undermining efforts to combat climate change and protect public health.

Financial and Reputational Fallout:

The fallout from the emissions scandal was severe for Volkswagen, resulting in significant financial and reputational damage. The company faced billions of dollars in fines, legal settlements, and recall costs related to the scandal. Volkswagen's stock price plummeted, erasing billions of dollars in shareholder value, and the company's brand reputation took a massive hit. The scandal also led to the resignation of Volkswagen's CEO and other top executives, further highlighting the magnitude of the crisis.

Rebuilding Trust and Remediation Efforts:

In the aftermath of the emissions scandal, Volkswagen embarked on a series of efforts to rebuild trust and address the damage caused by its deception. The company issued apologies to consumers and regulators, implemented recalls and software fixes for affected vehicles, and committed to transitioning to electric vehicles as part of its future strategy. Volkswagen also faced increased regulatory scrutiny and oversight, leading to reforms in emissions testing procedures and greater transparency in automotive manufacturing.

Lessons Learned and Industry Impact:

The Volkswagen emissions scandal served as a wake-up call for the automotive industry and regulators alike, highlighting the need for stricter oversight and accountability in emissions testing and compliance. The scandal prompted regulatory reforms and increased scrutiny of emissions standards, leading to stricter enforcement measures and greater transparency in emissions reporting. The Volkswagen case also underscored the importance of corporate integrity and ethical behavior in maintaining consumer trust and brand reputation, serving as a cautionary tale for companies across industries about the consequences of deception and betrayal of trust.

The chapter titled "Hypocrisy Toll: Brand Implosion Unveiled" delves into the critical importance of alignment between stated beliefs and actions in maintaining the integrity and sustainability of organizations, businesses, and families. It emphasizes that behavior, not mere belief, defines a brand's identity and reputation, and any disconnect between professed values and actual behavior leads to hypocrisy, eroding trust and credibility.

The chapter provides examples of both successful and failed companies to illustrate this principle. Companies like Patagonia, Ben & Jerry's, and TOMS are highlighted as exemplars of aligned behavior, where their commitment to environmental sustainability, social responsibility, and philanthropy is seamlessly integrated into their operations. Conversely, companies like Wells Fargo, Enron, and Volkswagen suffered severe consequences due to misalignment between their professed values and unethical practices.

The text emphasizes the far-reaching impact of such misalignment, including loss of customer trust, financial decline, and reputational damage. It underscores the importance of transparency, accountability, and ethical leadership in upholding organizational integrity and rebuilding trust in the aftermath of a crisis.

Key Points from the Chapter "Hypocrisy's Toll: Brand Implosion Unveiled":

1. Behavior is paramount in branding, as actions speak louder than beliefs, and any misalignment between professed values and actual behavior can lead to hypocrisy.

2. Hypocrisy, caused by behavior contradicting beliefs, can lead to the downfall of organizations, businesses, and families by eroding trust and damaging reputation.

3. Consistent and authentic behavior is crucial for building and maintaining trust in both personal and professional contexts.

4. Examples like Patagonia and Ben & Jerry's demonstrate successful brand identities built on consistent alignment of actions with stated values.

5. Misalignment between belief and action poses a grave threat to the stability and sustainability of any entity, ultimately resulting in its collapse.

6. Integrity is crucial for organizations, as stakeholders expect congruence between an entity's mission statement and its daily operations.

7. Today's consumers scrutinize businesses' actions, holding them accountable for discrepancies between stated values and behavior.

8. Families also rely on alignment between actions and beliefs to maintain trust and cohesion.

9. Examples like Wells Fargo demonstrate the damaging consequences of misaligned behavior on reputation and viability.

10. TOMS exemplifies how businesses can drive positive social change through innovative models like the "One for One" concept.

11. Misaligned behavior can lead to public backlash, loss of customer loyalty, negative publicity, and financial decline.

12. Ensuring consistency between declared values and real-world actions is critical for the sustainability and integrity of any entity.

Chapter 6

Bob Marley's Wisdom Navigating Life's Rat Race

Bob Marley's poignant lyrics resonate as a profound commentary on the human experience. "In the abundance of water, the fool is thirsty," encapsulates the irony of overlooking abundant resources while chasing elusive desires. The concept extends to the rat race, highlighting the futility of blindly pursuing societal expectations without true fulfillment.

C R Wallace

Bob Marley's lyrical wisdom delves into the paradox of human behavior, using the metaphor of a fool remaining thirsty in the abundance of water. This poignant insight extends beyond literal thirst, becoming a powerful commentary on the tendency to overlook abundant opportunities or resources while relentlessly pursuing ephemeral desires. The analogy is seamlessly woven into a broader societal critique, shedding light on the pitfalls of mindlessly engaging in the rat race without attaining genuine fulfillment.

Ephemeral desires, as illuminated by Marley's lyrics, symbolize transient and fleeting wishes that often captivate individuals. In the pursuit of these short-lived aspirations, people may inadvertently neglect substantial opportunities and resources surrounding them. Marley's message resonates by emphasizing the consequences of prioritizing momentary gratifications over long-term fulfillment, serving as a cautionary tale against the pitfalls of a life driven solely by superficial ambitions within the relentless rat race.

Marley's wisdom suggests that true contentment and meaning are found not in the relentless chase of fleeting desires but in recognizing and valuing the abundance already present in one's life. This perspective urges a shift in focus from external validation and material gain to inner peace and substantial personal growth. By highlighting this dichotomy, Marley's lyrics challenge listeners to reassess their priorities, encouraging a deeper understanding of what constitutes true wealth and happiness.

Moreover, this critique extends to societal norms and values that often equate success with material prosperity and social status. Marley's metaphor serves as a reminder that such measures of success are superficial and can lead to a hollow existence. Instead, he advocates for a more holistic approach to life, where fulfillment is derived from meaningful relationships, personal growth, and a sense of community.

In essence, Marley's lyrical metaphor of the thirsty fool in a land of water is a profound meditation on the human condition. It challenges individuals to transcend the superficial and embrace a more meaningful and abundant life, filled with genuine connections and lasting contentment.

The Thirst of the Fool in Abundance:

Consider a person surrounded by opportunities and resources but who remains oblivious to them, constantly seeking fulfillment in external pursuits. This metaphorical fool, thirsty amid the abundance of water, symbolizes those who overlook the richness of life's offerings, blinded by misplaced priorities.

This metaphor extends into various facets of the human experience. In personal relationships, for instance, one might neglect the deep connections and support systems readily available, choosing instead to chase superficial social validations or fleeting romances. Similarly, in the professional realm, individuals often pursue career milestones and material success at the expense of personal well-being and genuine satisfaction. This relentless pursuit of external markers of success leads to a hollow existence, where true contentment remains perpetually out of reach.

Moreover, the metaphor highlights the societal tendency to undervalue readily available resources and opportunities. Education, community, nature, and health are often underappreciated in favor of the pursuit of wealth, status, and consumer goods. People may find themselves caught in a cycle of working harder for more possessions and recognition, while neglecting the simpler, more enduring sources of happiness and fulfillment.

The "fool" in this metaphor is not inherently ignorant but rather misled by societal norms and pressures that dictate what is considered valuable or worthy of pursuit. This misalignment results in a life driven by ephemeral desires, those that are transient and often unfulfilling in the long run.

To transcend this cycle, a shift in perspective is necessary. Recognizing and appreciating the abundance already present in one's life can lead to a more fulfilling and balanced existence. This involves cultivating gratitude, nurturing relationships, and engaging in activities that foster personal growth and well-being. By realigning priorities, individuals can move from a state of perpetual thirst to one of satisfaction and contentment.

In essence, the "Thirst of the Fool in Abundance" is a call to awaken the wealth of opportunities and resources around us. It encourages a reassessment of what truly matters, urging us to seek fulfillment in the intrinsic rather than the extrinsic. Through this lens, Marley's wisdom serves as a timeless reminder to embrace a life rich in meaning, connection, and genuine happiness.

The Rat Race Disgrace:

Bob Marley's phrase "rat race, it's a disgrace to see the human race in a rat race" exposes the dehumanizing nature of a relentless pursuit without purpose. The rat race often involves chasing material success without considering the impact on one's well-being or relationships.

Marley's critique of the "rat race" goes beyond mere observation, shedding light on its dehumanizing effects. The phrase "it's a disgrace to see the human race in a rat race" unveils the inherent cost of relentless pursuits devoid of purpose. This race, often centered around material success, tends to neglect the crucial aspects of well-being and meaningful relationships. Marley's words serve as a stark reminder of the perilous consequences when individuals become entangled in a pursuit that sacrifices their humanity for the elusive goal of material gain.

The "rat race" metaphor vividly illustrates the monotonous and exhausting cycle of striving for societal definitions of success. Participants in this race often measure their worth through external achievements, such as job titles, financial status, and material possessions. This relentless drive can lead to significant personal costs, including stress, burnout, and a sense of emptiness. The pursuit of these extrinsic goals can overshadow intrinsic values like personal fulfillment, happiness, and connection with others.

Moreover, the rat race fosters a competitive environment where individuals are pitted against each other in a zero-sum game. This competition can erode community bonds and promote a culture of individualism and self-interest. In such a scenario, cooperation and mutual support are often sacrificed, leading to a fragmented society where genuine human connections are rare.

Marley's insight encourages a revaluation of what constitutes true success. Instead of being trapped in the cycle of accumulation and comparison, he urges a focus on holistic well-being. This includes nurturing relationships, engaging in meaningful work, and maintaining a balanced life. By emphasizing the importance of inner peace and satisfaction, Marley's critique advocates for a shift away from materialism towards a more human-centered approach to living.

The societal implications of the rat race are profound. It perpetuates inequality and social stratification, as not everyone has equal access to the means of achieving material success. This disparity can lead to widespread dissatisfaction and a sense of injustice, further fueling the cycle of relentless pursuit and discontent. Marley's words challenge us to recognize these broader impacts and consider how our personal choices contribute to this dynamic.

In essence, "The Rat Race Disgrace" is a call to break free from the confines of a life driven by superficial goals. Marley's wisdom highlights the need for a more balanced and fulfilling approach to life, one that values human connections, personal well-being, and meaningful achievements over mere material gain. By doing so, we can reclaim our humanity and find true contentment beyond the confines of the rat race.

The Unfulfilling Pursuit:

Imagine individuals sacrificing personal happiness, relationships, and well-being in pursuit of societal expectations. The disgrace lies in participating in a rat race that leads to stress, burnout, and a hollow sense of accomplishment. The human race, caught in this cycle, may find themselves questioning the true meaning of their pursuits.

In the relentless pursuit of societal expectations, individuals may unwittingly sacrifice personal happiness, strain relationships, and compromise their well-being. The disgrace of participating in such a rat race manifests in the toll it takes—leading to stress, burnout, and a hollow sense of accomplishment. As the human race becomes ensnared in this cycle, questions about the true meaning of their pursuits arise, unraveling the superficiality of societal norms and prompting reflection on the authentic sources of fulfillment often overshadowed by the demands of conformity.

This unfulfilling pursuit often begins with the pressure to meet societal standards of success, which are typically defined by external markers such as wealth, status, and material possessions. Individuals driven by these external expectations may find themselves in a constant state of competition, always striving for more but never truly satisfied. This cycle can lead to chronic stress and burnout, as the relentless demands of the rat race leave little room for rest or introspection.

The impact on personal relationships is also profound. The pursuit of societal approval often requires significant time and energy, which can detract from nurturing meaningful connections with family and friends. Relationships may suffer as individuals prioritize their careers or social standing over the people who matter most to them. This neglect can lead to feelings of isolation and loneliness, further exacerbating the sense of emptiness that accompanies the rat race.

Moreover, the focus on external achievements can cause individuals to overlook or undervalue their internal well-being. Mental health can deteriorate as the pressures of maintaining a certain image or lifestyle become overwhelming. Physical health may also be compromised, as long hours and high stress levels take their toll. In the end, the pursuit of societal expectations often results in a hollow sense of accomplishment, where the external success achieved does not translate into genuine happiness or fulfillment.

Bob Marley's wisdom challenges us to break free from the foolish thirst for abundance and the disgraceful rat race. By recognizing the abundance around us and evaluating our pursuits, we can navigate life with a sense of purpose and fulfillment rather than being blinded by the illusion of scarcity or the societal rat race.

Marley's wisdom serves as a call to liberation from both the foolish thirst amidst abundance and the disgraceful rat race. It urges us to shift our perspective, acknowledging the abundance surrounding us, and prompting a revaluation of our pursuits. By doing so, we can navigate life with a renewed sense of purpose and fulfillment, escaping the illusion of scarcity and the pressures of societal expectations. Marley's insight encourages a mindful approach to life, fostering a journey guided by authenticity rather than being ensnared by the misguided pursuits that often lead to discontent.

In essence, breaking free from these cycles requires a conscious effort to prioritize what truly matters—inner peace, meaningful relationships, and personal well-being. It involves questioning societal norms and redefining success in terms that resonate with our true selves. By doing so, we can find lasting happiness and a deeper sense of purpose, creating a life that is rich in genuine fulfillment rather than superficial accomplishments.

In conclusion, Bob Marley's lyrical wisdom serves as a beacon guiding readers away from the pitfalls of the rat race and the folly of overlooking abundance. His profound insights remind us to seek fulfillment in meaningful pursuits rather than chasing ephemeral desires or societal expectations blindly. By embracing the rich-ness of life's offerings and nurturing authentic connections, we can navigate the journey with purpose, escaping the dehumanizing grasp of the rat race and finding true fulfillment along the way. Bob Mar-ley's legacy transcends music, offering timeless wisdom that reso-nates deeply with the human experience, urging us to live deliber-ately and authentically.

Key Points from "Bob Marley's Wisdom Navigating Life's Rat Race"

1. Abundant Resources Overlooked:

Bob Marley's lyrics "In the abundance of water, the fool is thirsty" highlight the irony of ignoring plentiful resources while chasing elusive desires.

2. Ephemeral Desires:

Marley criticizes the pursuit of fleeting, superficial aspirations that often lead to neglect of substantial opportunities and resources.

3. True Fulfillment:

Marley's wisdom suggests that real contentment comes from recognizing and valuing the abundance already present in one's life rather than seeking external validation and material gain.

4. Critique of Societal Norms:

Marley's lyrics challenge societal values that equate success with material prosperity and social status, highlighting their superficial nature and potential to lead to hollow lives.

5. Human Connections and Personal Growth:

True wealth and happiness are found in meaningful relationships, personal growth, and community, as opposed to material accumulation.

6. The "Thirst of the Fool" Metaphor:

This metaphor emphasizes the tendency to overlook life's riches while being blinded by misplaced priorities, applicable in personal and professional contexts.

7. Rat Race Disgrace:

Marley's phrase, "rat race, it's a disgrace to see the human race in a rat race," critiques the dehumanizing effects of the relentless pursuit of material success without regard for well-being or relationships.

8. Impact on Well-being:

The rat race leads to stress, burnout, and a hollow sense of accomplishment, often causing individuals to question the true meaning of their pursuits.

9. Competitive Environment:

The rat race fosters competition and individualism, eroding community bonds and mutual support, and promoting a culture of self-interest.

10. Holistic Well-being:

Marley advocates for a balanced life focused on nurturing relationships, engaging in meaningful work, and maintaining inner peace, as opposed to mere material gain.

11. Societal Implications:

The rat race perpetuates inequality and social stratification, leading to widespread dissatisfaction and a sense of injustice.

12. Call to Reevaluate Pursuits:

Marley encourages a reassessment of what truly matters, advocating for fulfillment in intrinsic values rather than societal expectations.

13. Mindful Approach to Life:

By recognizing the abundance around us and shifting our focus to what truly matters, individuals can achieve a sense of purpose and genuine fulfillment.

14. Breaking Free from Cycles:

Escaping the cycles of superficial pursuits requires prioritizing inner peace, meaningful relationships, and personal well-being, and redefining success in terms that resonate with our true selves.

15. Timeless Wisdom:

Marley's insights offer timeless guidance, urging us to seek fulfillment in meaningful pursuits and authentic connections, and to live deliberately and authentically.

16. Legacy Beyond Music:

Bob Marley's legacy extends beyond his music, providing profound commentary on the human experience and guiding readers away from the pitfalls of the rat race towards a more fulfilling life.

Chapter 7

Biblical Insights on Anger Management and Communication

Mastering Emotional Intelligence: The Iron-Striking Analogy

"Unless you want to break the iron, it's not always wise to strike when the iron is hot. When dealing with a situation where we are burning with anger, it's not the moment to strike."

C R Wallace

The scriptures state:

James 1:19-21 New King James Version (NKJV)

"So then, my beloved brethren, let every man be swift to hear, slow to speak, slow to wrath; for the wrath of man does not produce the righteousness of God."

We have one mouth and two ears; we should listen to others at least two times as much as we speak. Proverb 17:28 states: "Even fools are thought wise if they keep silent, and discerning if they hold their tongues."

The quote emphasizes the importance of patience, restraint,

and effective communication, drawing wisdom from both life experience and biblical teachings.

In life's complex tapestry, we frequently find ourselves at the mercy of intense emotions like anger or frustration, compelling us to respond impulsively. Yet, akin to the delicate art of blacksmithing, where striking iron when it's too hot risks its very integrity, yielding to anger can fracture the bonds of our relationships and tarnish our interactions with others.

Embedded within the sacred verses of James 1:19-21 lies a timeless blueprint for navigating life's tempestuous seas of emotion. It beckons us to embody the virtues of attentive listening, measured speech, and restrained anger. This divine counsel serves as a gentle yet profound reminder to approach life's trials with grace and wisdom, resisting the urge to succumb to the fiery impulses of anger. By embracing the discipline of active listening and judiciously tempering our responses, we unlock the transformative power of understanding, reconciliation, and righteousness, illuminating the path toward harmonious coexistence and spiritual fulfillment.

A poignant biblical example illustrating the consequences of yielding to anger can be found in the story of Moses. Despite his faithful service and leadership, Moses was ultimately barred from entering the Promised Land because of a moment of uncontrolled anger. In Numbers 20:10-12, Moses, frustrated with the Israelites' constant complaints, struck a rock twice to bring forth water instead of speaking to it as God had commanded. This act of disobedience, fueled by his anger, led to God's decision to deny him entry into the Promised Land. Moses' experience serves as a powerful reminder of the profound impact that uncontrolled anger can have on our lives and destinies.

Furthermore, Proverb 17:28 unveils the profound significance of silence and restraint in the intricate tapestry of communication. It unveils the paradoxical truth that even those devoid of wisdom can don the cloak of sagacity by embracing the virtue of silence and withholding their tongues. This sacred revelation serves as a poignant reminder of the transformative potential inherent in thoughtful reflection and discernment before uttering a single word. It extols the virtues of patient listening and keen observation as indispensable tools in navigating the complexities of human interaction. Through the practice of intentional silence and judicious restraint, we unlock the gateway to deeper understanding, enhanced discernment, and profound interpersonal connection, ultimately enriching the fabric of our shared existence with wisdom and grace.

Subtitle: "Practical Applications of Biblical Wisdom in Everyday Life"

In both life experiences and biblical wisdom, we find valuable insights into anger management and effective communication.

Let's delve into some examples:

In practical terms, these biblical principles can be applied to various aspects of life. For example, in a heated argument with a loved one, instead of lashing out in anger, taking a moment to listen attentively to their perspective can promote empathy and understanding. Similarly, in a professional setting, exercising restraint and thoughtfulness in communication can foster productive dialogue and conflict resolution.

In practical terms, the timeless wisdom encapsulated in these biblical principles transcends the boundaries of religious doctrine, offering invaluable guidance for navigating the complexities of everyday life. Consider a heated argument with a loved one, where emotions run high and tempers flare. Rather than succumbing to the impulse to retaliate with anger, pausing to engage in active listening can serve as a powerful antidote. By attentively tuning in to the perspective of our loved one, we open the door to empathy and mutual understanding, laying the groundwork for constructive dialogue and heartfelt reconciliation.

Similarly, in the realm of professional interactions, the application of restraint and thoughtfulness in communication holds the key to unlocking the potential for growth and collaboration. Picture a tense meeting where divergent viewpoints clash, threatening to derail progress and breed animosity. By exercising deliberate restraint in our speech and embodying the spirit of James 1:19-21, we cultivate an environment conducive to productive dialogue and conflict resolution. Through the art of measured speech and patient listening, we foster a culture of respect, trust, and cooperation, enabling us to navigate challenges with grace and fortitude.

The Story of Moses:

A vivid biblical example illustrating the consequences of unchecked anger is the story of Moses in Numbers 20:10-12. Despite his faithful service, Moses allowed his frustration with the Israelites to lead him into disobedience. Instead of speaking to the rock to bring forth water as God commanded, Moses struck it twice. This act of anger and disobedience cost Moses dearly, resulting in God forbidding him from entering the Promised Land. This story underscores the importance of controlling our emotions.

In essence, the practical application of these biblical principles serves as a compass guiding us through the ebb and flow of life's myriad encounters. Whether in moments of interpersonal strife or professional discord, the virtues of swift listening, measured speech, and restrained anger illuminate the path toward harmony, understanding, and righteousness. By embracing these timeless precepts with humility and intentionality, we embark on a journey toward personal growth, relational flourishing, and profound spiritual fulfillment.

Overall, the profound insights gleaned from biblical teachings on anger management and communication offer a timeless roadmap for steering through the intricate tapestry of human interactions. As we weave these principles into the fabric of our lives, we unlock the potential to transform the way we relate to others, fostering deeper connections and fostering a harmonious coexistence.

By embracing the wisdom encapsulated in passages like James 1:19-21 and Proverb 17:28, we embark on a journey of self-discovery and relational enrichment. These scriptures beckon us to embody virtues such as patience, empathy, and self-restraint, guiding us towards a more enlightened way of engaging with the world around us.

Through intentional practice and reflection, we can harness the power of active listening and measured speech to defuse conflicts, bridge divides, and cultivate an atmosphere of mutual respect and understanding. In doing so, we not only elevate the quality of our personal relationships but also contribute to the collective well-being of our communities and society at large.

Moreover, by internalizing these timeless precepts and allowing them to permeate every facet of our being, we pave the path towards righteousness in our words and actions. As we strive to embody the virtues of humility, compassion, and forgiveness, we become beacons of light, illuminating the darkness with the transformative power of love and grace.

In essence, the integration of biblical insights into our daily lives holds the promise of profound spiritual growth and relational flourishing. By heeding the wisdom of ages past and applying it with wisdom and discernment, we unlock the door to a future characterized by deeper connections, greater harmony, and a steadfast commitment to righteousness in all that we do.

Subtitle: "Practical Applications of Biblical Wisdom in Everyday Life"

In both life experiences and biblical wisdom, we find valuable insights into anger management and effective communication. Let's delve into some examples:

1. Patience in Conflict Resolution:

Consider the scenario where a colleague's mistake at work triggers a surge of frustration and anger. In the heat of the moment, reacting impulsively by confronting them might exacerbate tensions and jeopardize the professional relationship. However, by applying the timeless wisdom of "not striking when the iron is hot," we afford ourselves the opportunity for a calmer, more deliberate response. This principle resonates deeply with the biblical injunction from James 1:19-21, which exhorts us to exercise patience in the face of conflict, advocating for a measured approach to communication that fosters understanding and reconciliation. By embodying this virtue, we not only navigate workplace challenges more effectively but also demonstrate our commitment to honoring biblical principles in our professional conduct.

2. The Power of Listening:

Picture a family gathering where tensions simmer beneath the surface, ready to ignite with the spark of differing opinions. Instead of plunging headlong into arguments or heated debates, embracing the power of attentive listening can transform the dynamic. As Proverb 17:28 astutely observes, "Even fools are thought wise if they keep silent, and discerning if they hold their tongues." This sage advice underscores the profound impact of silent observation and thoughtful reflection in diffusing conflicts. By lending an ear to each person's perspective and resisting the urge to offer immediate retorts, we create space for understanding and empathy to flourish. In doing so, we embody the essence of the biblical principle of being "swift to hear, slow to speak," paving the way for genuine dialogue, thus fostering reconciliation and harmony in familial relationships.

3. Reflection on Personal Growth:

Reflecting on personal growth often brings to mind moments when acting impulsively leads to regrettable outcomes in relationships or interactions. These experiences teach us the profound value of self-restraint and thoughtful communication. Consider a time when a hasty, angry response caused a rift with a friend or colleague. By learning from such moments, we can appreciate the importance of pausing and reflecting before reacting. This pause allows us to consider the potential consequences of our words and actions, leading to more constructive and peaceful resolutions. The wisdom of not acting on anger impulsively is deeply rooted in biblical teachings, such as those found in James 1:19-21, which emphasize the virtues of patience, active listening, and measured speech. By embracing these principles, we align ourselves with the pursuit of righteousness and peace, fostering healthier and more harmonious relationships. This approach not only aids in conflict resolution but also promotes personal growth, as we become more mindful and deliberate in our interactions, cultivating a character marked by wisdom and integrity.

4. The Story of Moses:

A vivid biblical example illustrating the consequences of unchecked anger is the story of Moses in Numbers 20:10-12. Despite his faithful service, Moses allowed his frustration with the Israelites to lead him into disobedience. Instead of speaking to the rock to bring forth water as God commanded, Moses struck it twice. This act of anger and disobedience cost Moses dearly, resulting in God forbidding him from entering the Promised Land. This story underscores the importance of controlling our emotions.

In essence, these examples illustrate how biblical insights on anger management and communication resonate with practical life experiences. By embracing patience, active listening, and self-control, we navigate conflicts more effectively, foster healthier relationships, and ultimately strive towards embodying the righteousness of God in our interactions with others.

In conclusion, the chapter on Biblical Insights on Anger Management and Communication highlights the timeless wisdom found in both scripture and personal experience. Through the metaphorical advice of not striking the iron when it's hot and the biblical teachings of being swift to listen and slow to anger, we are reminded of the importance of patience and restraint in our interactions.

By incorporating these principles into our lives, we can navigate conflicts more effectively and cultivate healthier relationships. Whether it's pausing before reacting in anger or actively listening to others with empathy and understanding, the guidance provided by scripture offers practical solutions to everyday challenges.

Furthermore, the chapter emphasizes the power of reflection and personal growth. Learning from past experiences and striving for self-improvement allows us to embody the righteousness of God in our words and actions.

In essence, by applying the insights gleaned from both life

experiences and biblical wisdom, we can enhance our communication skills, promote harmony in our relationships, and journey towards a more fulfilling and righteous way of living.

Key Takeaways:

1. Importance of Patience and Restraint:

The quote underscores the significance of exercising patience and restraint in moments of anger or frustration. Just as striking the iron when it's too hot can lead to breakage, reacting impulsively in anger can have harmful consequences in relationships and interactions.

2. Biblical Guidance on Communication:

Drawing from James 1:19-21, the chapter emphasizes the biblical teaching to be swift to listen, slow to speak, and slow to anger. This counsel encourages a thoughtful and discerning approach to communication, promoting understanding, reconciliation, and righteousness.

3. Value of Silence and Listening:

Proverb 17:28 highlights the power of silence and listening in communication. Even fools can appear wise when they choose to keep silent and hold their tongues. This biblical insight underscores the importance of active listening and thoughtful reflection before speaking.

4. The Story of Moses:

Moses' experience in Numbers 20:10-12 serves as a profound lesson in the consequences of uncontrolled anger. Despite his long-standing leadership and faithfulness, Moses' moment of anger, where he struck the rock instead of speaking to it as God commanded, resulted in God denying him entry into the Promised Land. This story illustrates the critical importance of managing anger and adhering to God's instructions, as failing to do so can lead to significant repercussions.

5. Practical Applications in Daily Life:

The chapter provides practical examples of applying biblical principles to everyday situations. From conflict resolution in the workplace to navigating family gatherings, embracing patience, active listening, and self-control enhances communication effectiveness and fosters healthier relationships.

6. Emphasis on Personal Growth and Reflection:

Reflecting on past experiences and striving for self-improvement allows individuals to embody righteousness in their interactions. Learning from mistakes and practicing patience and restraint contribute to personal growth and relational harmony.

Overall, the chapter highlights the timeless wisdom found in both scripture and personal experience, offering practical guidance for managing anger and improving communication in various aspects of life.

Chapter 8
Shades of Unity: Embracing Diversity in the Garden of Life

The chapter "Shades of Unity: Embracing Diversity in the Garden of Life" beautifully illustrates the importance of celebrating diversity and promoting unity in the human experience.

In the garden of life, a plethora of flowers blooms, each displaying a unique array of colors. We marvel at the diverse species of flowers and their different hues. However, within humanity, some choose to denigrate those who possess a different color or shade. Instead, why not celebrate and appreciate those who differ from us in color or shade? Unity triumphs over brutality.

C R Wallace

"Shades of Unity: Embracing Diversity in the Garden of Life" encapsulates the essence of celebrating diversity and promoting unity. Let's explore this concept further with some real-life examples:

Cultural diversity is not just a fact of life; it's a source of richness and vitality that enhances the human experience. Just as a garden flourishes with a variety of flowers, humanity flourishes with the diversity of cultures, traditions, and languages that color our world. Embracing cultural diversity goes beyond mere tolerance;

it's about actively seeking to understand and appreciate the differences that make each culture unique.

When we embrace cultural diversity, we open ourselves up to a world of learning and enrichment. Each culture offers its own perspective on life, values, and traditions, providing valuable insights and lessons that can broaden our horizons and deepen our understanding of the world around us. By engaging with different cultures, we cultivate empathy, compassion, and respect for others, fostering a more inclusive and harmonious society.

Cultural festivals, such as Diwali, Christmas, or Eid, provide wonderful opportunities for people from diverse backgrounds to come together and celebrate their shared humanity. These celebrations not only showcase the beauty of various cultural traditions but also serve as powerful reminders of our common bonds and shared values. Whether it's gathering with family and friends to exchange gifts, feast on traditional foods, or participate in religious ceremonies, cultural festivals offer moments of joy, connection, and unity that transcend cultural differences.

Moreover, embracing cultural diversity promotes social cohesion and harmony within communities. By fostering an environment of inclusivity and acceptance, we create spaces where people of all backgrounds feel valued and respected. This, in turn, strengthens social bonds and builds bridges between individuals and communities, leading to greater cooperation, collaboration, and mutual understanding.

In today's interconnected world, where globalization has made diversity an integral part of everyday life, embracing cultural diversity is more important than ever. It allows us to navigate the complexities of our increasingly diverse societies with grace and understanding, paving the way for a future where differences are celebrated, and diversity is seen as a source of strength and resilience.

In conclusion, cultural diversity is not only a fundamental aspect of human existence but also a powerful force for positive change. By embracing and celebrating the richness of our cultural tapestry, we can create a more inclusive, compassionate, and harmonious world for generations to come.

Racial harmony is not just about coexistence; it's about embracing the beauty and richness that comes from the diversity of human races, much like the vibrant array of colors found in a garden of flowers. Just as each flower contributes to the overall beauty of the garden, each race adds its unique hue to the tapestry of humanity. Embracing racial diversity means going beyond mere tolerance to actively recognizing and celebrating the value that each race brings to our collective experience.

Initiatives promoting racial harmony play a crucial role in

fostering understanding, empathy, and solidarity among people of different racial backgrounds. Multicultural festivals, for example, provide vibrant showcases of diverse cultural traditions, art forms, and cuisines, offering opportunities for individuals to learn about and appreciate the customs and heritage of others. By participating in these festivals, people can celebrate the beauty of racial diversity while forging connections and building relationships across racial lines.

Community dialogues and discussions are another important avenue for promoting racial harmony. These forums create safe spaces for individuals to engage in open and honest conversations about race, identity, privilege, and discrimination. Through respectful dialogue and active listening, participants can gain a deeper understanding of the lived experiences and perspectives of people from different racial backgrounds, fostering empathy, compassion, and mutual respect.

Education also plays a vital role in promoting racial harmony by challenging stereotypes, biases, and prejudices that perpetuate racial inequality and division. By incorporating diverse perspectives and histories into school curricula, educators can help students develop a more nuanced understanding of race and its impact on society. Moreover, promoting diversity and inclusion in educational institutions cultivates environments where students from all racial backgrounds feel valued, respected, and empowered to succeed.

Beyond individual and community-level efforts, policies and initiatives at the institutional and governmental levels are essential for addressing systemic racism and promoting racial equity. This includes measures to ensure equal access to education, healthcare, employment, housing, and justice for all racial groups. By dismantling barriers and addressing disparities, policymakers can create more inclusive and equitable societies where everyone has the opportunity to thrive, regardless of their race or ethnicity.

Ultimately, achieving racial harmony requires collective action and commitment from individuals, communities, and institutions alike. By embracing and celebrating racial diversity, fostering dialogue and understanding, and advocating for policies that promote racial equity, we can create a world where every individual is valued, respected, and treated with dignity, regardless of their race or ethnicity. In this way, we can cultivate a garden of racial harmony where the beauty of diversity blooms and flourishes for generations to come.

In the garden of life, diversity encompasses not only differences in race, culture, and tradition but also includes individuals with disabilities, each bringing their own unique abilities and perspectives to the tapestry of humanity. Embracing this diversity means going beyond mere tolerance to actively create inclusive environments where everyone, regardless of their abilities, feels valued, respected, and empowered to participate fully in society.

Implementing accessibility measures is crucial for ensuring that individuals with disabilities can navigate and engage with their surroundings effectively. This includes physical accommodations such as ramps, elevators, and wheelchair-accessible facilities in public spaces, workplaces, and educational institutions. By removing barriers to access, these measures enable individuals with disabilities to participate in everyday activities, pursue education and employment opportunities, and contribute their talents and skills to their communities.

However, inclusion goes beyond just physical accessibility; it also involves fostering a culture of acceptance, understanding, and support for individuals with disabilities. This requires challenging stereotypes, biases, and misconceptions about disability and recognizing the inherent value and dignity of every individual, regardless of their abilities. Creating inclusive communities involves promoting empathy, compassion, and respect for people with disabilities, as well as providing opportunities for meaningful engagement and social connection.

Inclusive education is a fundamental aspect of fostering inclusion and empowerment for individuals with disabilities. By providing access to quality education and support services, educational institutions can empower students with disabilities to reach their full potential, develop essential skills, and pursue their academic and career goals. Inclusive education benefits not only students with disabilities but also promotes diversity and enriches the learning experience for all students by fostering understanding, empathy, and appreciation for differences.

Employment is another key domain where the inclusion of individuals with disabilities is essential. By implementing inclusive hiring practices, providing reasonable accommodations, and fostering supportive work environments, employers can tap into the unique talents and perspectives of individuals with disabilities, driving innovation, creativity, and diversity in the workplace. Moreover, promoting diversity and inclusion in the workforce benefits businesses by enhancing employee morale, productivity, and customer satisfaction.

Inclusive policies and initiatives at the governmental and institutional levels are critical for advancing the rights and opportunities of individuals with disabilities. This includes legislation such as the Americans with Disabilities Act (ADA) in the United States, which prohibits discrimination against individuals with disabilities and mandates accessibility in public accommodations, employment, transportation, and telecommunications. Governments and organizations must also invest in programs and services that support the inclusion and empowerment of individuals with disabilities, such as vocational rehabilitation, assistive technology, and community-based support services.

Ultimately, creating a truly inclusive society requires collective action and commitment from individuals, communities, and institutions to dismantle barriers, challenge stereotypes, and promote acceptance and understanding of individuals with disabilities. By embracing diversity in all its forms, including disability, we can cultivate a garden of inclusion where every individual is valued, respected, and empowered to thrive. In this way, we can build a more equitable, accessible, and inclusive world where everyone has the opportunity to reach their full potential and contribute their unique gifts to the greater good.

In the vibrant garden of life, where diversity blooms in myriad colors and forms, there are, unfortunately, instances where the petals of prejudice and discrimination cast shadows over the beauty of difference. Yet, amidst these challenges, the seeds of unity and understanding can flourish, offering hope for a more harmonious society.

Embracing diversity and promoting unity are powerful antidotes to the poison of prejudice and discrimination. By recognizing and celebrating the richness of human diversity, we can transcend barriers of race, ethnicity, religion, gender, and socioeconomic status, forging connections that bridge divides and nurture a sense of shared humanity.

Community outreach programs play a crucial role in sowing the seeds of social harmony and unity. These initiatives bring together individuals from diverse backgrounds, providing opportunities for dialogue, collaboration, and mutual learning. Through workshops, cultural exchanges, and collaborative projects, community members can gain insights into different perspectives, challenge stereotypes, and build relationships based on empathy, respect, and understanding.

Empathy lies at the heart of social harmony, enabling individuals to connect with others on a deeper level, to walk in their shoes, and to recognize their common humanity. Through empathy, we can overcome fear and prejudice, cultivate compassion and solidarity, and create communities where everyone feels valued, included, and supported.

Respect is another essential pillar of social harmony, reflecting a recognition of the inherent worth and dignity of every individual. By treating others with respect, regardless of their background or identity, we can foster an environment of trust, cooperation, and mutual respect, laying the foundation for a more inclusive and equitable society.

Understanding is the fruit of empathy and respect, enabling individuals to appreciate the complexities of human experience and the nuances of different cultures, traditions, and perspectives. Through dialogue and education, we can broaden our horizons, challenge our assumptions, and cultivate a culture of curiosity, openness, and lifelong learning.

Together, empathy, respect, and understanding form the bedrock of social harmony, fostering relationships built on trust, compassion, and mutual respect. By embracing diversity, promoting unity, and standing together against prejudice and discrimination, we can create communities where everyone feels valued, accepted, and empowered to contribute their unique gifts to the collective tapestry of humanity. In this way, we can nurture a garden of social harmony, where the flowers of diversity bloom in vibrant harmony, and the seeds of unity take root and flourish.

In each of these examples, embracing diversity and promoting unity leads to a more vibrant, inclusive, and harmonious society. By celebrating the unique qualities and contributions of every individual, regardless of differences, we cultivate a garden of life where unity truly triumphs over brutality.

Now, let's highlight some famous individuals in history who

have made a positive impact on the human experience, contributing to the garden of life:

1. Nelson Mandela:

A towering figure in the fight against apartheid in South Africa, Mandela spent 27 years in prison for his activism before becoming the country's first black president. He advocated for reconciliation and forgiveness, leading efforts to dismantle institutionalized racism and establish a democratic and inclusive society.

2. Martin Luther King Jr:

A prominent leader in the American civil rights movement, King championed equality, justice, and nonviolent protest. His stirring speeches and peaceful activism played a crucial role in ending segregation and advancing civil rights legislation, inspiring generations to fight for racial equality and social justice.

3. Malala Yousafzai:

A fearless advocate for girls' education and human rights, Malala defied the Taliban in her native Pakistan and survived an assassination attempt at the age of 15. Despite facing adversity, she continues to campaign globally for the right to education for all children, becoming the youngest-ever Nobel Prize laureate.

4. Albert Einstein:

Renowned for his groundbreaking theories in physics, Einstein's intellectual contributions revolutionized our understanding of the universe. Beyond his scientific achievements, he was also an outspoken advocate for peace, human rights, and social justice, using his platform to promote global cooperation and understanding.

5. Rosa Parks:

Often referred to as the "Mother of the Civil Rights Movement," Parks played a pivotal role in challenging racial segregation in the United States. Her refusal to give up her bus seat to a white passenger sparked the Montgomery Bus Boycott, a key event in the struggle for racial equality and civil rights.

6. Wangari Maathai:

A Kenyan environmentalist and political activist, Maathai founded the Green Belt Movement, focusing on tree planting, environmental conservation, and women's rights. She was the first African woman to receive the Nobel Peace Prize for her contribution to sustainable development, democracy, and peace.

7. Desmond Tutu:

A South African Anglican bishop and social rights activist, Tutu was a key figure in the fight against apartheid. He promoted nonviolent protest and reconciliation and chaired the Truth and Reconciliation Commission, helping to heal a divided nation through truth-telling and forgiveness.

These individuals, among many others, have left an indelible mark on history through their courage, compassion, and dedication to making the world a better place. Their actions and teachings continue to inspire and uplift humanity, enriching the garden of life with hope, resilience, and progress.

Famous Individuals' Contributions

Highlighting the positive impact of historical figures such as Nelson Mandela, Martin Luther King Jr., Malala Yousafzai, Albert Einstein, Rosa Parks, Wangari Maathai, and Desmond Tutu, who have made significant contributions to humanity through their courage, compassion, and dedication to promoting unity and celebrating diversity.

Overall, embracing diversity and promoting unity leads to a more vibrant, inclusive, and harmonious society where unity triumphs over brutality.

The chapter "Shades of Unity: Embracing Diversity in the Garden of Life" eloquently underscores the significance of celebrating diversity and fostering unity in the human experience. By likening humanity to a garden teeming with a diverse array of flowers, each displaying its unique colors, the chapter poignantly calls attention to the beauty found in differences.

Through real-life examples, the chapter vividly illustrates the importance of embracing diversity across various aspects of life. From cultural celebrations that bridge communities to initiatives promoting racial harmony and inclusive environments for individuals with disabilities, the message is clear: unity thrives when diversity is celebrated and embraced.

Moreover, the chapter challenges the notion of denigrating others based on differences and instead advocates for a culture of appreciation and respect for diversity. By promoting social harmony through empathy, understanding, and community outreach, we can create a more inclusive and harmonious society where unity triumphs over prejudice and discrimination.

In addition, the chapter pays homage to famous individuals throughout history who have made profound contributions to humanity by championing unity and celebrating diversity. From Martin Luther King Jr.'s philosophy of nonviolent resistance to Rosa Parks' pivotal role in challenging racial segregation, these figures serve as beacons of inspiration, reminding us of the transformative power of courage, compassion, and dedication to social justice.

In conclusion, "Shades of Unity: Embracing Diversity in the Garden of Life" urges us to embrace diversity as a source of strength and richness in the fabric of humanity. By fostering unity through appreciation, respect, and understanding of differences, we can cultivate a garden of life where every individual is valued and celebrated for their unique contribution to the tapestry of human existence.

Main takeaways from the chapter "Shades of Unity: Embracing Diversity in the Garden of Life":

1. Celebrating Cultural Diversity:

Embracing the multitude of cultures, traditions, and languages enriches humanity, fostering understanding and unity.

2. Valuing Racial Harmony:

Recognizing and appreciating the beauty of racial diversity promotes understanding and builds bridges across communities.

3. Promoting Inclusion of Individuals with Disabilities:

Creating inclusive environments where everyone feels valued and respected enhances societal diversity and ensures that everyone can contribute their talents.

4. Advocating for Social Harmony:

Overcoming prejudice and discrimination through empathy, respect, and understanding fosters social unity and inclusivity.

Chapter 9

Deflecting Projections: Embracing Self-Reflection

We must not be on the screen of other people's projections. Reject their projections with a mindset of deflection by having the right reflection of who we are regardless of their goals and objectives to defame our name.

C R Wallace

Letting them know their opinions will not shape our opinion of ourselves will make their false sense of control mesmerize their soul when they realize they have no control over your soul.

In life, there will be individuals who believe they have the right to control your soul. When confronted with this situation, avoid confrontation and go in the other direction to protect your soul. Your peace is what brings solace to your soul, so don't oblige them by giving them a piece of your mind, which would be unkind and disrupt your peace of mind.

When faced with such individuals, I urge you to remember that silence is golden. It prevents you from adding fuel to their fire as they try to gaslight you. These liars will attempt to humiliate you, using their hate to denigrate you due to their own insecurities. They will try to impose a false identity on you because of their distorted perception of reality.

Maintaining your silence in these moments is not a sign of weakness but a powerful assertion of your strength and control over your own inner peace. Responding to their provocations only gives them the power they seek over you. Instead, by choosing not to engage, you maintain your dignity and keep your emotional well-being intact.

Remember, the goal of these individuals is often to drag you down to their level of negativity and chaos. By refusing to respond, you deny them this victory. You preserve your energy and focus on what truly matters in your life. It's essential to recognize that their attempts to control or belittle you stem from their own unresolved issues and insecurities. Their distorted view of reality is a reflection of their inner turmoil, not a truth about you.

So, walk away and protect your peace. Your soul is precious, and maintaining its tranquility should be your priority. In silence, you find the strength to rise above their negativity, and in doing so, you set a powerful example for others to follow.

Remove yourself from such circles, be it friends or family. For your sanity, you must face the reality that the person you have control over is you, no need to engage, things will only disintegrate, leaving you feeling out of place.

We must decide in our minds that true peace is worth more

than anything we can attain, be it fortune, fame, marital or professional status. These are things many people trade their peace of mind to attain.

From my experience, I will encourage you to refrain from exchanging these things for a peaceful existence.

Peace of mind is a divine experience; don't let anyone take it from you. Surrendering your peace would be akin to gaining the world at the expense of losing your soul.

When someone tries to disturb your peace, remember that their actions are often projections of their own inner turmoil. The best remedy to maintain a peaceful state of mind is to reflect these projections by going in the other direction.

Choosing to walk away is not an act of cowardice but a profound demonstration of self-respect and wisdom. It means recognizing that your inner tranquility is too valuable to be sacrificed for the fleeting satisfaction of responding to negativity. In this way, you safeguard your soul from the corrosive effects of anger and resentment.

Embrace the power of silence. In moments of provocation, silence can be your greatest ally. It shields you from the toxicity others try to impose and allows you to stay grounded in your own truth. By not engaging, you preserve your mental and emotional well-being, which is essential for leading a balanced and fulfilling life.

It's also important to cultivate self-awareness and self-compassion. Understand that you are not responsible for others' insecurities or distorted views. Their attempts to impose a false identity on you are merely reflections of their internal struggles. By maintaining a clear boundary between their issues and your own sense of self, you can remain unaffected by their attempts to disrupt your peace. In this journey of protecting your peace of mind, practice mindfulness and self-care. Engage in activities that nourish your soul and bring you joy. Surround yourself with positive influences and supportive relationships that uplift you. This holistic approach to maintaining peace ensures that you are resilient in the face of negativity and can continue to thrive despite external challenges.

Ultimately, protecting your peace of mind is about valuing yourself and prioritizing your well-being. It's about making conscious choices that align with your highest good and refusing to let anyone diminish your sense of inner harmony. By doing so, you not only preserve your peace but also inspire others to do the same.

In a world where external opinions often overshadow my inner voice, I have come to understand the importance of deflecting projections and embracing self-reflection. As I reflect on my own words, "I must not be the screen of other people's projections," I realize the profound truth in reclaiming my own narrative and identity.

Rejecting these projections demands a steadfast mindset grounded in self-awareness and confidence. It starts with recognizing that the opinions and judgments of others are often more about them than they are about me. People project their insecurities, fears, and unresolved issues onto others, creating a distorted reflection that has little to do with my true self.

To effectively deflect these projections, I must cultivate a deep understanding of who I am. This involves continuous self-reflection and an honest evaluation of my strengths, weaknesses, values, and beliefs. By building a strong sense of self, I create a foundation that is resilient against external influences. I become less susceptible to the negative opinions and more attuned to my inner voice, which guides me toward my authentic path.

Confidence plays a crucial role in this process. It empowers me to trust my own perceptions and judgments over the unsolicited opinions of others. Confidence is not about arrogance or dismissing feedback; it's about discerning constructive criticism from destructive negativity and choosing what serves my growth and well-being.

This journey of self-discovery and self-acceptance is not without its challenges. There will be moments of doubt and pressure to conform to others' expectations. However, by remaining committed to my truth, I can navigate these challenges with resilience and grace. This commitment means standing firm in my identity, even when faced with attempts to defame or undermine my character.

Self-reflection is a powerful tool in this journey. It allows me to assess situations objectively, understand my reactions, and learn from my experiences. Through self-reflection, I gain insights into my behavior patterns and emotional triggers, enabling me to respond rather than react to external provocations.

Ultimately, rejecting others' projections and embracing self-reflection is about reclaiming my narrative. It's about deciding who I am based on my own understanding and not on the distorted views imposed by others. This reclamation is an act of self-love and empowerment, allowing me to live authentically and confidently.

By embracing this mindset, I not only protect my peace but also inspire others to do the same. My journey becomes a beacon of resilience and authenticity, demonstrating that true strength lies in knowing and being oneself, despite the noise and pressure of the external world.

Readers can benefit from my experience by developing self-awareness and building confidence, which helps in recognizing and deflecting others' projections. Embracing self-reflection allows for a better understanding of one's reactions to external pressures. Establishing boundaries is crucial for protecting one's peace, while prioritizing self-care strengthens resilience against negativity. Staying true to core values guides decisions and actions, enabling individuals to navigate life with integrity and authenticity. By sharing my journey and the lessons I've learned, I hope to empower readers to embark on their own paths of self-discovery and self-acceptance, reclaiming their narratives and maintaining peace of mind amidst external noise.

Yet, this journey is not without its obstacles. Along the way, I encounter individuals who seek to control my thoughts and actions. Whether through manipulation, gaslighting, or attempts at humiliation, these individuals challenge my sense of self-worth and identity. However, I've learned that silence can be my most potent weapon in such situations. By refusing to engage in their toxic narratives, I reclaim my power and protect my peace of mind.

Moreover, I've realized the importance of prioritizing my well-being by distancing myself from toxic relationships and environments. Whether it's friends, family, or social circles, I understand that my sanity and growth come first. As I wisely note, "the person I have control over is me." By acknowledging my agency and choosing to walk away from negativity, I create space for personal growth and healing.

Readers can benefit from my experience by developing self-awareness and building confidence, which helps in recognizing and deflecting others' projections. Embracing self-reflection allows for a better understanding of one's reactions to external pressures. Establishing boundaries is crucial for protecting one's peace, while prioritizing self-care strengthens resilience against negativity. Staying true to core values guides decisions and actions, enabling individuals to navigate life with integrity and authenticity. By sharing my journey and the lessons I've learned, I hope to empower readers to embark on their own paths of self-discovery and self-acceptance, reclaiming their narratives and maintaining peace of mind amidst external noise.

Ultimately, my pursuit of true peace transcends external validation or material success. While fame, fortune, and status may offer temporary gratification, they pale in comparison to the profound serenity that comes from aligning with my authentic self. As I journey forward, I prioritize inner harmony and resist the temptation to sacrifice my peace of mind for external accolades.

Ultimately, my pursuit of true peace transcends external validation or material success. While fame, fortune, and status may offer temporary gratification, they pale in comparison to the profound serenity that comes from aligning with my authentic self. As I journey forward, I prioritize inner harmony and resist the temptation to sacrifice my peace of mind for external accolades.

In essence, my journey of deflecting projections and embracing self-reflection is a profound act of self-love and empowerment. It's a testament to my resilience and capacity for growth, even in the face of adversity. So, I heed my own words and remember that true peace resides within me, waiting to be discovered amidst life's tumultuous currents. I encourage you to join me on this journey of self-liberation.

"Deflecting Projections: Embracing Self-Reflection" by C R Wallace

C R Wallace's chapter "Deflecting Projections: Embracing Self-Reflection" provides a profound exploration of how to protect one's inner peace from external negativity. The central theme emphasizes rejecting others' projections and instead fostering a deep self-awareness and confidence to maintain emotional and mental well-being.

Wallace begins by addressing the phenomenon of projections, where individuals project their insecurities, fears, and unresolved issues onto others. These projections can distort one's self-perception and disrupt inner peace. To counteract this, Wallace advocates for a mindset of deflection, rooted in a clear understanding of one's true identity. This involves steadfast self-reflection and the rejection of external attempts to defame or control one's sense of self.

A key strategy Wallace highlights is maintaining silence in the face of provocation. He argues that silence is not a sign of weakness but a powerful assertion of strength. By refusing to engage with those who seek to gaslight or humiliate, individuals preserve their dignity and mental well-being. Silence prevents adding fuel to the fire and helps in avoiding unnecessary confrontations that only serve to empower the provocateur.

Wallace underscores the importance of prioritizing peace of mind over external validation or material success. True peace, he asserts, is more valuable than fame, fortune, or professional status. The temptation to sacrifice inner tranquility for these external rewards should be resisted. Instead, individuals should cultivate self-awareness and self-compassion, recognizing that others' negative perceptions are reflections of their own inner turmoil rather than truths about themselves.

To further protect one's peace, Wallace advises distancing oneself from toxic relationships and environments. Whether these are friends, family, or social circles, it's essential to recognize the importance of one's sanity and growth. By choosing to walk away from negativity, individuals create space for personal development and healing.

Wallace also emphasizes the role of mindfulness and self-care in maintaining peace of mind. Engaging in activities that nourish the soul and surrounding oneself with positive influences can bolster resilience against external challenges. This holistic approach ensures that one remains grounded and focused on what truly matters in life.

In conclusion, Wallace's chapter is a call to action for readers to reclaim their narratives through self-reflection and deflection of negative projections. By doing so, individuals can maintain their inner peace, live authentically, and inspire others to do the same. The journey of self-discovery and self-acceptance, though challenging, is ultimately a path to true serenity and empowerment. Wallace's message is clear: prioritize inner harmony and refuse to let external negativity disrupt your peace of mind.

Key points from the chapter "Deflecting Projections: Embracing Self-Reflection" by C R Wallace:

1. Rejecting Projections:

Do not accept others' projections of their insecurities and unresolved issues onto you.

2. Self-Reflection:

Cultivate a deep understanding of who you are through continuous self-reflection and honest self-evaluation.

3. Maintaining Silence:

Use silence as a powerful tool to avoid engaging with provocations and to protect your peace.

4. Prioritizing Inner Peace:

Value inner tranquility above external validation, material success, or societal expectations.

5. Distancing from Toxicity:

Remove yourself from toxic relationships and environments to safeguard your mental and emotional well-being.

6. Confidence and Self-Awareness:

Develop confidence and self-awareness to recognize and deflect negative opinions and judgments from others.

7. Mindfulness and Self-Care:

Engage in activities that nourish your soul and surround yourself with positive influences to maintain resilience.

8. Understanding Projections:

Recognize that others' negative perceptions and attempts to control you are reflections of their inner turmoil, not truths about you.

9. Setting Boundaries:

Establish and maintain clear boundaries to protect your peace and prevent others from imposing their issues on you.

10. Living Authentically:

Stay true to your core values and live authentically, despite external pressures and negativity.

11. Empowering Others:

By reclaiming your narrative and maintaining your peace, you set an example and inspire others to do the same.

12. Self-Love and Empowerment:

Embrace self-love and empowerment as essential elements of protecting your peace and living a fulfilling life.

13. Navigating Challenges with Grace:

Face challenges with resilience and grace, standing firm in your identity and refusing to conform to others' distorted views.

Chapter 10
The Truth behind the Saying: Happy Wife, Happy Life

Behind Closed Doors:

Exploring the True Meaning of Happiness in Marriage, we have all heard the saying, "Happy wife, happy life." However, this is a fable. The truth is that a happy home is the prerequisite for a happy life. The happiness of a home can only be sustained with a harmonious relationship between spouses. If there is an imbalance of love and respect in the union, it will eventually lead to a breakdown, often resulting in separation and divorce due to the stress and imbalance in the relationship.

C R Wallace

Chapter: The Perils of the "Happy Wife, Happy Life" Myth

Introduction:

The Allure and Pitfalls of a Popular Myth

The saying "Happy wife, happy life" has echoed through generations as a mantra for successful marriages. Yet, beneath its seemingly harmless surface lies a myriad of potential dangers. In this chapter, we'll uncover the perils of subscribing to this myth and the toll it can take on relationships.

Unrealistic Expectations:

The widely embraced adage "Happy wife, happy life" has been woven into the fabric of marital advice for generations. While on the surface, it may appear as a lighthearted guideline for a harmonious union, a deeper exploration reveals a host of potential pitfalls that can adversely impact relationships.

One of the most significant dangers of the "Happy wife, happy life" myth is the burden of unrealistic expectations it places on husbands. It implies that a husband's primary duty is to ensure his wife's happiness at all times. This can lead to immense pressure and feelings of inadequacy when these expectations prove impossible to meet consistently. Such a mindset can create a dynamic where the husband's needs and emotions are sidelined, fostering resentment and emotional imbalance in the relationship.

Furthermore, this adage perpetuates a simplistic and one-dimensional view of marital satisfaction, ignoring the complex, reciprocal nature of a healthy partnership. It suggests that the wife's happiness is the sole barometer of the marriage's success, overshadowing the importance of mutual satisfaction, communication, and emotional support. A thriving relationship requires both partners to actively engage in fostering each other's well-being, rather than one person bearing the responsibility for the other's happiness.

The myth also risks reinforcing outdated gender roles, where the husband is seen as the provider and protector and the wife as the recipient of care and attention. This can inhibit genuine emotional intimacy and partnership, as it places both spouses into rigid, stereotypical roles that may not align with their true selves or the dynamics of modern relationships. Couples may find themselves trapped in these roles, unable to communicate their true needs and desires, ultimately leading to dissatisfaction and disconnection.

Moreover, the "Happy wife, happy life" mantra can mask deeper issues within the marriage. If a husband's sole focus becomes keeping his wife happy, underlying problems such as poor communication, unmet needs, or personal growth can be ignored or suppressed. This approach can prevent couples from addressing and resolving conflicts constructively, which is essential for long-term relational health and satisfaction.

In addition, the pressure to constantly make one's spouse happy can lead to burnout and emotional exhaustion. Husbands might feel they need to continually sacrifice their own happiness and well-being to fulfill this role, which is neither sustainable nor healthy. Over time, this can lead to feelings of resentment, frustration, and a diminished sense of self-worth.

For a more balanced and fulfilling relationship, it is crucial for both partners to recognize the importance of mutual support, respect, and communication. Happiness should be a shared responsibility, with both individuals contributing to and benefiting from the relationship's emotional and psychological richness. This involves open dialogue about each partner's needs and expectations, fostering an environment where both can thrive.

Ultimately, dispelling the "Happy wife, happy life" myth involves embracing a more nuanced understanding of marital happiness. By acknowledging that both partners' happiness is vital, couples can work towards a more equitable and satisfying relationship, where both individuals feel valued, heard, and supported. This shift in perspective encourages a deeper connection and a more resilient partnership, capable of weathering the inevitable challenges that life brings.

Consider a scenario where the sole focus is on ensuring the wife's happiness at the expense of the husband's well-being. This approach might lead to unspoken expectations and unaddressed needs, fostering an imbalance that could strain the relationship. The undue pressure to single-handedly uphold the happiness of the spouse might create an environment where genuine communication and mutual understanding take a back seat.

In this dynamic, the husband may feel compelled to suppress

his own emotions and desires to prioritize his wife's happiness, leading to a sense of emotional neglect or invisibility. This can breed resentment and erode trust, as the husband may feel his needs are not valued or respected within the relationship. Over time, this imbalance can create a rift between partners, hindering intimacy and connection.

Furthermore, the "Happy wife, happy life" mantra can inadvertently perpetuate gender stereotypes, reinforcing the notion that a woman's happiness is the linchpin for a successful marriage. Such an outlook may overlook the individual complexities and needs of both partners, limiting the depth and authenticity of their connection.

This narrow focus on the wife's happiness may also stifle the husband's emotional expression, as he may feel pressured to conform to traditional masculine ideals of strength and stoicism. As a result, important conversations about emotional needs, desires, and vulnerabilities may go unexplored, further deepening the emotional disconnect between partners.

Moreover, this mindset can create unrealistic expectations for the wife, placing an undue burden on her to fulfill the role of the sole source of happiness within the relationship. This pressure can be overwhelming and isolating, as the wife may feel responsible for her husband's emotional well-being while neglecting her own needs.

To cultivate a more balanced and fulfilling relationship, it is essential for both partners to prioritize open communication, mutual respect, and empathy. This involves acknowledging and validating each other's emotions, needs, and desires, without falling into restrictive gender roles or outdated stereotypes.

By shifting the focus from individual happiness to mutual well-being, couples can create a more equitable and resilient partnership, where both partners feel seen, heard, and valued. This approach fosters a deeper connection and intimacy, as partners work together to navigate life's challenges and celebrate each other's joys. Ultimately, by embracing a more inclusive and compassionate understanding of marital happiness, couples can build a foundation of trust, love, and mutual support that withstands the test of time.

In the pursuit of prioritizing one person's happiness over the collective well-being of the partnership, couples might find themselves navigating a delicate tightrope. Sacrifices made solely to appease one partner could lead to resentment or unmet expectations, eroding the foundation of a healthy and thriving relationship.

Consider the scenario where a husband constantly puts his wife's happiness above his own, sacrificing his own needs and desires in the process. While this may initially seem selfless and noble, it can create an imbalance within the relationship. The husband may begin to feel overlooked or unappreciated, leading to feelings of resentment or frustration over time. Similarly, the wife may feel burdened by the responsibility of her husband's happiness, struggling to meet unrealistic expectations while neglecting her own well-being.

This imbalance can manifest in various aspects of the relationship, from decision-making and communication to intimacy and emotional support. When one partner's needs consistently take precedence over the other's, it can create tension and discord, undermining the trust and intimacy that are essential for a strong bond.

Furthermore, sacrificing one's own happiness for the sake of the other can perpetuate a cycle of dependency and enablement. The partner whose happiness is prioritized may come to rely on the other to fulfill their emotional needs, rather than cultivating their own sense of fulfillment and self-worth. This dynamic can hinder personal growth and autonomy, as individuals become increasingly dependent on their partner for validation and happiness.

In essence, this chapter aims to unravel the layers of the "Happy wife, happy life" mantra, using real-life examples to illustrate its potential dangers. By examining these intricacies, it seeks to provide a nuanced understanding of the dynamics within marriages, urging for a more balanced and holistic approach to fostering happiness and fulfillment for both spouses.

By acknowledging and addressing the complexities inherent in relationships, couples can cultivate a partnership based on mutual respect, support, and understanding. This involves prioritizing open communication, empathy, and compromise, while also recognizing and honoring each other's individuality and autonomy. In doing so, couples can create a relationship that is built on a foundation of trust, love, and shared happiness, enriching their lives and strengthening their bond for years to come.

Building on a False Premise:

When a relationship is built upon the false premise that one partner's happiness should be the sole focus, it lays a shaky foundation. True partnerships are based on mutual respect, shared happiness, and the understanding that both individuals contribute to the relationship's well-being. The "Happy wife, happy life" myth obscures this fundamental truth.

Imagine a scenario where the "Happy wife, happy life" mantra dominates a relationship. Jack, wanting to adhere to this popular advice, consistently prioritizes Jill's happiness above all else. He plans elaborate surprises, caters to her every need, and ensures her comfort without addressing his own desires or concerns. On the surface, it may seem like a devoted gesture, but beneath lies a brewing imbalance.

In this dynamic, Jack's constant focus on Jill's happiness neglects his own emotional well-being. Over time, unspoken expectations build up, and Jack may find himself sacrificing personal goals or suppressing genuine feelings to maintain the illusion of a perpetually happy wife. The foundation of their relationship becomes shaky as Jack's authentic self remains unexpressed, and the connection lacks the depth that comes from both partners contributing to each other's happiness.

Moreover, the imbalance created by prioritizing one partner's happiness over the other's can lead to resentment and dissatisfaction. Jack may harbor feelings of neglect or frustration, resenting the expectation placed upon him to constantly cater to Jill's needs without receiving reciprocal care and consideration. Meanwhile, Jill may feel suffocated by the pressure to maintain a facade of happiness, unable to express her own desires or vulnerabilities for fear of disappointing Jack.

As the relationship continues to unfold, the cracks in the foundation become more pronounced. Communication becomes strained, as Jack and Jill struggle to express their true feelings and needs openly. Trust erodes, as each partner begins to question the authenticity of the other's actions and intentions. Ultimately, the relationship may reach a breaking point, as the imbalance created by the "Happy wife, happy life" myth becomes too great to sustain.

To avoid such pitfalls, it is essential for couples to recognize and challenge the false premise underlying the "Happy wife, happy life" mantra. Instead of prioritizing one partner's happiness at the expense of the other, couples should strive for mutual fulfillment and shared responsibility. This involves open communication, active listening, and a willingness to compromise and support each other's growth and well-being.

By embracing a more balanced and equitable approach to relationships, couples can build a foundation of trust, respect, and love that withstands the test of time. Each partner's happiness is valued and prioritized, leading to a relationship that is grounded in authenticity, connection, and mutual happiness.

Contrast this with a couple, Chris and Jen, who approach their relationship with a more realistic perspective. They understand that happiness is multifaceted and influenced by various factors, not solely dependent on one partner's actions. When challenges arise, they tackle them together, acknowledging that supporting each other during tough times is an integral part of a genuine connection.

In the face of life's inevitable ups and downs, the couple remains resilient. Rather than harboring disappointment when happiness wavers, they embrace the shared journey, recognizing that navigating challenges together strengthens their bond.

Chris and Jen's relationship serves as a beacon of resilience and authenticity amidst the sea of idealized expectations. By acknowledging the complexity of happiness and the importance of shared responsibility, they create a solid foundation for their partnership to thrive.

Their approach contrasts starkly with the rigid confines of the "Happy wife, happy life" myth. Instead of placing undue pressure on one partner to uphold the other's happiness, Chris and Jen distribute the responsibility evenly, recognizing that true happiness emerges from a deep connection and mutual support.

Ultimately, by embracing a shared responsibility for each other's happiness and well-being, couples can forge a relationship that withstands the test of time. Chris and Jen's journey serves as a testament to the power of authenticity, resilience, and mutual support in creating a fulfilling and enduring partnership. They communicate openly about their desires, dreams, and even challenges. Each takes responsibility for contributing to the other's well-being, fostering an environment of mutual respect. If Chis has a goal or dream, Jen actively supports and participates in its realization, creating a reciprocal exchange of joy and fulfillment.

In this context, the couple thrives on the understanding that both partners play an essential role in the relationship's health. The happiness of one doesn't overshadow the importance of the other's contentment. It's a dynamic built on equality and shared responsibility, contrasting starkly with the potentially precarious imbalance fueled by the "Happy wife, happy life" myth. Chris and Jen's relationship serves as a compelling example of the power of partnership grounded in mutual support and understanding. By prioritizing open communication and actively participating in each other's lives, they create a strong foundation of trust, respect, and love.

In contrast, the imbalance inherent in the "Happy wife, happy life" myth can lead to resentment, dissatisfaction, and, ultimately, the erosion of the relationship. When one partner's happiness is prioritized at the expense of the other, it creates an unsustainable dynamic where one individual feels overlooked or undervalued.

Therefore, the essence of a robust and enduring relationship lies in acknowledging that both individuals contribute to the partnership's happiness. This chapter aims to shed light on the pitfalls of an approach that places undue emphasis on the happiness of one partner, emphasizing the need for a more holistic and balanced perspective in fostering a truly fulfilling and sustainable connection.

Ultimately, by embracing a shared responsibility for each other's happiness and well-being, couples can create a relationship that thrives on mutual respect, support, and love. It's not about sacrificing one's own happiness for the sake of the other, but rather, finding joy and fulfillment in supporting each other's growth and happiness. This shift in perspective fosters a deeper connection and a stronger bond, ensuring that the relationship remains fulfilling and enduring for years to come.

Acknowledging Fear:

In this context, the couple thrives on the understanding that both partners play an essential role in the relationship's health. The happiness of one doesn't overshadow the importance of the other's contentment. It's a dynamic built on equality and shared responsibility, contrasting starkly with the potentially precarious imbalance fueled by the "Happy wife, happy life" myth.

Chris and Jen's relationship serves as a compelling example of the power of partnership grounded in mutual support and understanding. By prioritizing open communication and actively participating in each other's lives, they create a strong foundation of trust, respect, and love.

In contrast, the imbalance inherent in the "Happy wife, happy life" myth can lead to resentment, dissatisfaction, and, ultimately, the erosion of the relationship. When one partner's happiness is prioritized at the expense of the others, it creates an unsustainable dynamic where one individual feels overlooked or undervalued.

Therefore, the essence of a robust and enduring relationship lies in acknowledging that both individuals contribute to the partnership's happiness. This chapter aims to shed light on the pitfalls of an approach that places undue emphasis on the happiness of one partner, emphasizing the need for a more holistic and balanced perspective in fostering a truly fulfilling and sustainable connection.

Ultimately, by embracing a shared responsibility for each other's happiness and well-being, couples can create a relationship that thrives on mutual respect, support, and love. It's not about sacrificing one's own happiness for the sake of the other, but rather, finding joy and fulfillment in supporting each other's growth and happiness. This shift in perspective fosters a deeper connection and a stronger bond, ensuring that the relationship remains fulfilling and enduring for years to come.

The Disappointment of Reality:

Reality has a way of challenging even the most ingrained beliefs. When a husband realizes that he cannot always maintain his wife's happiness, disappointment can set in. This disappointment can be a catalyst for conflict, resentment, and, ultimately, relationship breakdowns.

Consider Mark, a devoted husband who wholeheartedly embraced the "Happy wife, happy life" mantra. He dedicated himself to creating an environment where his wife, Sarah, should, in theory, be constantly happy. Mark meticulously planned romantic gestures, attended to household chores, and prioritized Sarah's preferences in every decision. However, despite his sincere efforts, there were moments when Sarah experienced natural fluctuations in her mood or faced external stressors that Mark couldn't control.

In this scenario, the realization hit Mark hard—that, despite his best intentions, he couldn't guarantee Sarah's perpetual happiness. The belief he held so fervently began to crumble in the face of the unpredictability of life. This realization planted seeds of disappointment, both in himself for not living up to the ideal, and potentially in Sarah, who might have felt pressured to conform to an unrealistic expectation.

As the pressure to maintain an always-happy wife intensified, so did the conflicts. Mark's disappointment transformed into frustration, and Sarah, feeling the weight of unrealistic expectations, may have started resenting the idea that her happiness defined the entirety of their relationship. This disillusionment could serve as a catalyst for communication breakdowns, arguments, and, in extreme cases, the deterioration of the relationship.

The disappointment of reality underscores the danger of basing a relationship on an unrealistic premise. When individuals realize that their efforts to uphold an idealized version of their partner's happiness are unsustainable, it can lead to feelings of inadequacy, frustration, and disillusionment. This, in turn, can strain the bond between partners, eroding trust and intimacy.

Moreover, the disappointment experienced by both partners highlights the importance of realistic expectations and open communication in a healthy relationship. Rather than striving for an unattainable standard of constant happiness, couples should focus on supporting each other through life's ups and downs, acknowledging that moments of joy and sorrow are inevitable.

By embracing the reality of imperfection and vulnerability, couples can cultivate a deeper sense of connection and resilience in their relationship. This involves recognizing and accepting each other's humanity, with all its flaws and complexities, and offering unconditional love and support. In doing so, couples can navigate the challenges of life together, strengthening their bond and building a foundation of trust and mutual respect that withstands the test of time.

In contrast, Chris and Jen, who approach their relationship with a more realistic perspective. They understand that happiness is multifaceted and influenced by various factors, not solely dependent on one partner's actions. When challenges arise, they tackle them together, acknowledging that supporting each other during tough times is an integral part of a genuine connection.

In the face of life's inevitable ups and downs, the couple remains resilient. Rather than harboring disappointment when happiness wavers, they embrace the shared journey, recognizing that navigating challenges together strengthens their bond. The myth of "Happy wife, happy life" can set unrealistic expectations and, when confronted with the complexities of reality, lead to a cascade of negative consequences within a relationship.

A Breaking Point:

The weight of trying to adhere to the myths of unrealistic standards can lead to a breaking point in a marriage. Feelings of frustration, exhaustion, and disillusionment can accumulate over time, eroding the very foundations of love and commitment that a healthy marriage requires.

Consider the case of Emma and Alex, a couple who initially embraced the "Happy wife, happy life" mantra with genuine intentions. Alex, driven by a desire to ensure Emma's constant happiness, went above and beyond to fulfill her every wish. He worked long hours to provide financial stability, surprised her with thoughtful gifts, and prioritized her needs over his own.

In the beginning, Emma appreciated the gestures, feeling momentarily content. However, as time passed, the weight of Alex's efforts began to take a toll. Emma, aware of the sacrifices Alex made, felt an increasing pressure to maintain a facade of perpetual happiness. The expectation that her well-being should be the sole focus of the relationship became stifling.

As Emma grappled with life's inevitable challenges—career stress, personal struggles, and the complexities of daily life—the facade crumbled. The unrealistic standards set by the "Happy wife, happy life" myth became apparent. Alex, despite his sincere efforts, couldn't shield Emma from the natural ebb and flow of emotions that come with being human.

The accumulation of pressure and the realization that sustaining constant happiness was an unattainable goal created a rift in their marriage. Emma, feeling burdened by the expectation to be endlessly happy, started to withdraw. Alex, despite his best intentions, found himself unable to meet the unrealistic standards he had set for himself.

The breaking point occurred when the strain on their relationship became too much to bear. Frustration, exhaustion, and disillusionment set in. Emma and Alex, once united by love and commitment, found themselves at odds with the very essence of their connection.

This example illustrates how the pursuit of an unattainable ideal, driven by the "Happy wife, happy life" myth, can lead to a breaking point in a marriage. The weight of unrealistic standards, coupled with the complexities of life, can erode the foundations of love and commitment, ultimately jeopardizing the well-being of the relationship.

The Need for Realistic Expectations:

In navigating the complexities of a marital relationship, it's essential to set realistic expectations. Happiness is a shared responsibility, and acknowledging the ebb and flow of emotions is a sign of emotional maturity. Partners should aspire to make each other happy but understand that both will experience moments of discontent.

Conclusion:

Redefining Relationship Success:

Ultimately, the "Happy wife, happy life" myth oversimplifies the intricate nature of a successful marriage. Healthy relationships thrive on mutual respect, shared happiness, and a deep understanding of each other's needs and emotions. It's vital to recognize that true happiness cannot be achieved by making one person responsible for another's emotional state. By redefining relationship success, couples can embrace the imperfections of life together, growing stronger through both joy and adversity.

The Imperfection of Constant Happiness:

Expecting anyone to make another person happy all the time is unrealistic and, in many cases, unattainable. Human emotions are complex and multifaceted, and everyone experiences moments of sadness, frustration, or stress. It's essential to recognize that true happiness doesn't mean being in a constant state of euphoria but rather weathering life's ups and downs together.

Self-Happiness vs. Fear:

The closing question invites reflection: "Are you truly happy, or are you scared?" This question delves into the concept of self-happiness and the role fear can play in a relationship. Happiness should never be compromised for fear of conflict or change.

The Importance of Self-Happiness:

Being content with oneself is a prerequisite for a happy relationship. Individuals who are secure in their own happiness can contribute positively to the happiness of their partners. In contrast, relying solely on a partner for one's happiness can lead to disappointment and strain.

Acknowledging Fear:

Fear can manifest in various ways within a relationship. It might be the fear of confrontation, the fear of change, or the fear of being alone. Acknowledging and addressing these fears is crucial for personal growth and the health of a partnership.

Key Points from the Chapter: 

1. Introduction:

The saying "Happy wife, happy life" is popular but hides potential dangers.

The chapter aims to explore the perils of this myth and its impact on relationships.

2. Unrealistic Expectations:

The myth places unrealistic expectations on husbands to prioritize their wife's happiness. It can lead to imbalance, gender stereotypes, and strain in relationships.

3. Building on a False Premise:

Relationships should be based on mutual respect and shared happiness, not a one-sided focus. Examples contrast the imbalance of the myth with the equality of shared happiness.

4. The Disappointment of Reality:

Unrealistic expectations can lead to disappointment and conflict. Realistic couples acknowledge life's challenges and support each other.

5. A Breaking Point:

The pursuit of constant happiness can lead to relationship breakdowns.

Unrealistic standards create pressure and disillusion-ment.

6. **The Need for Realistic Expectations:**
    Partners should set realistic expectations and understand the ebb and flow of emotions.

Conclusion:

Redefining Relationship Success:

True happiness in a relationship comes from mutual respect and understanding.

The myth oversimplifies the complexities of marriage.

The Imperfection of Constant Happiness:

Expecting constant happiness is unrealistic; true happiness involves facing life's challenges together.

Self-Happiness vs. Fear:

Happiness should not be compromised by fear of conflict or change.

The Importance of Self-Happiness:

Being content with oneself is essential for a happy relation-ship.

Chapter 11

Embracing Progression - Over Perfection

Moving Forward: The Antidote to Regressive Perfectionism

Progression over perfection will lead you in the right direction. Seeking perfection without forward progression will lead you to a life of regression, where your gifts never find expression.

C. R. Wallace

Introduction:

In a world that often glorifies perfection, it's easy to fall into the trap of striving for flawlessness at any cost. However, as C. R. Wallace wisely points out, progression over perfection is the key to unlocking our true potential. In this chapter, we will explore the transformative power of embracing progression over perfection and how it can lead us to a life of fulfillment and expression. We'll also draw inspiration from the lives of notable figures who have embodied this principle, including a famous Black inventor and a biblical example.

The Pitfalls of Regressive Perfectionism:

Regressive perfectionism, characterized by an obsessive

pursuit of flawlessness and an overwhelming fear of failure, can severely impact our well-being and success. This mindset breeds a paralyzing fear of making mistakes, leading to an inability to move forward or take risks. Consequently, individuals become trapped in a cycle of stagnation, missed opportunities, and ultimately, a life of regret. Understanding the lived experiences of those who have struggled with regressive perfectionism can provide deeper insights into its detrimental effects and offer practical strategies for overcoming it.

The Nature of Regressive Perfectionism:

Regressive perfectionism is rooted in the belief that any deviation from perfection is unacceptable. This leads to an intense fear of failure and a constant need to meet impossibly high standards.

Individuals with this mindset often avoid taking on new challenges for fear of not excelling.

Procrastinate or delay completing tasks to avoid the possibility of making mistakes.

Experience significant stress and anxiety over minor errors or perceived imperfections. Become overly critical of themselves and others, fostering a negative and toxic environment.

Lived Experiences and Insights:

1. The Trap of Stagnation Lived Experience:

Consider Alex, a talented graphic designer who constantly sought perfection in every project. Alex would spend countless hours tweaking designs to achieve an elusive standard of flawlessness. This led to missed deadlines and a reluctance to take on new projects. Eventually, Alex's career stagnated, and opportunities for growth were lost.

Insight: The pursuit of perfection can create a paralyzing fear of progress, preventing individuals from seizing new opportunities and moving forward in their careers.

2. The Fear of Failure:

Lived Experience: Maria, an aspiring writer, dreamed of publishing a novel but was terrified of receiving negative feedback. She rewrote the first few chapters countless times, never feeling satisfied enough to submit her manuscript. Years passed, and Maria's novel remained unfinished, leaving her with a profound sense of regret.

Insight: The fear of failure can lead to a reluctance to take risks, resulting in missed opportunities and unfulfilled potential.

3. The Impact on Mental Health:

Lived Experience: James, a high-achieving student, pushed himself to maintain perfect grades. Any grade lower than an A caused him intense anxiety and self-doubt. The constant pressure led to burnout and depression, ultimately affecting his academic performance and overall well-being.

Insight: The constant pressure to be perfect can lead to severe mental health issues, including anxiety, depression, and burnout.

Recognizing Regressive Perfectionism:

To effectively recognize regressive perfectionism, look for these signs:

Procrastination:

Delaying tasks due to fear of not meeting high standards. Over-Preparation: Spending excessive time on minor details to avoid mistakes.

Avoidance:

Shying away from new opportunities or challenges to prevent failure.

Self-Criticism:

Being overly critical of oneself for minor errors or imperfections.

High Anxiety:

Experiencing significant stress and anxiety over tasks and

outcomes.

Managing Regressive Perfectionism:

Once you have identified regressive perfectionism, it is essential to manage it proactively to protect your emotional well-being.

1. Embrace Imperfection Strategy:

Accept that perfection is unattainable and that mistakes are a natural part of growth and learning.

Benefit: This mindset shift reduces the fear of failure and encourages a more realistic approach to tasks and challenges.

2. Set Realistic Goals Strategy:

Establish achievable and realistic goals that allow for flexibility and adjustment.

Benefit: Realistic goals reduce pressure and make it easier to progress without the need for perfection.

3. Practice Self-Compassion Strategy:

Treat yourself with kindness and understanding, especially when you make mistakes or face setbacks.

Benefit: Self-compassion fosters resilience and reduces the negative impact of self-criticism.

4. Focus on the Process Strategy:

Shift your focus from the end result to the process of learning and improvement.

Benefit: Emphasizing the journey rather than the destination encourages growth and reduces the obsession with flawless outcomes.

5. Seek Support Strategy:

Surround yourself with supportive individuals who understand your struggles and can offer encouragement.

Benefit: A supportive network provides a safety net during challenging times and reinforces positive changes.

Regressive perfectionism can lead to a cycle of stagnation, missed opportunities, and a life of regret. By recognizing the signs of this mindset and taking proactive steps to manage it, you can break free from the paralyzing fear of failure and embrace a more balanced and fulfilling approach to life. Drawing on lived experiences highlights the profound impact of regressive perfectionism and underscores the importance of cultivating self-compassion, setting realistic goals, and focusing on growth rather than perfection.

The Psychological Impact of Regressive Perfectionism:

Regressive perfectionism, characterized by the relentless pursuit of flawlessness and an overwhelming fear of failure, can have severe psychological impacts. This mindset places immense pressure on individuals to meet impossibly high standards, leading to significant stress and mental health issues. Understanding these impacts through the lens of lived experiences can provide deeper insights into the challenges faced by perfectionists and offer practical strategies for managing this harmful mindset.

The Toll on Mental Health:

1. Anxiety and Depression Lived Experience:

Consider Lisa, a high school student who excelled academically but constantly worried about maintaining her top grades. The fear of receiving anything less than an A caused her significant anxiety, leading to sleepless nights and an inability to enjoy her achievements. When she received a lower grade in a challenging course, Lisa fell into a deep depression, feeling like she had failed herself and her family.

Insight: The constant fear of not measuring up can lead to chronic anxiety and depression. The pressure to be perfect leaves little room for self-compassion, exacerbating feelings of inadequacy and failure.

2. **Erosion of Self-Esteem and Confidence Lived Experience:**

Mark, a talented musician, was praised for his performances but always felt that he could do better. He constantly compared himself to others and focused on his perceived shortcomings. Over time, this eroded his self-esteem and confidence. Despite his talent, Mark started to doubt his abilities and avoided auditions and opportunities that could advance his career.

Insight: The pressure to be perfect can erode self-esteem and confidence, making it difficult to take the necessary steps towards growth and improvement. The focus on flaws and failures overshadows achievements, leading to a diminished sense of self-worth.

3. **Paralysis by Analysis Lived Experience:**

Jane, a project manager, was known for her meticulous attention to detail. However, her perfectionism often led to overanalyzing every aspect of her projects. She would spend hours revising and rechecking her work, fearing any mistake could jeopardize the outcome. This not only delayed project timelines but also created immense stress and burnout.

Insight: Perfectionism can lead to paralysis by analysis, where the fear of making mistakes prevents individuals from making decisions or taking action. This constant scrutiny and self-doubt contribute to significant psychological stress and hinder productivity.

Recognizing the Psychological Impacts:

To effectively recognize the psychological impacts of regressive perfectionism, look for these signs:

Chronic Anxiety:

Persistent worry about meeting high standards and fear of failure.

Depressive Symptoms:

Feelings of hopelessness, lack of motivation, and sadness resulting from perceived failures.

Low Self-Esteem:

A diminished sense of self-worth and constant self-criticism.

Avoidance Behaviors:

Avoiding new challenges or opportunities due to fear of not being perfect.

Burnout:

Physical and emotional exhaustion from constant striving and stress.

Managing the Psychological Impacts:

Addressing the psychological impacts of regressive perfectionism requires proactive strategies to foster a healthier mindset and improve mental well-being.

1. **Embrace Imperfection Strategy:**

Accept that mistakes are a natural part of growth and learning. Acknowledge your efforts and achievements, even if they are not perfect.

Benefit: This reduces the fear of failure and promotes a more realistic and compassionate self-view.

2. **Set Realistic Expectations**

Strategy: Establish achievable goals and standards that allow for flexibility and adjustments. Recognize that perfection is unattainable and aim for progress instead.

Benefit: Setting realistic expectations reduces pressure and fosters a healthier approach to tasks and challenges.

3. **Practice Self-Compassion Strategy:**

Treat yourself with the same kindness and understanding you would offer a friend. Acknowledge your struggles and celebrate your successes.

Benefit: Self-compassion builds resilience and counteracts the negative effects of self-criticism.

4. Focus on the Process, Not the Outcome Strategy:

Shift your focus from the end result to the process of learning and improvement. Celebrate the effort and progress made rather than solely the outcome.

Benefit: Emphasizing the journey encourages growth and reduces the obsession with flawless results.

5. Seek Professional Help Strategy:

If perfectionism is significantly impacting your mental health, consider seeking support from a mental health professional. Therapy can provide tools and strategies to manage perfectionistic tendencies.

Benefit: Professional guidance can help address underlying issues and promote healthier coping mechanisms.

6. Build a Support Network Strategy:

Surround yourself with supportive individuals who understand your struggles and can offer encouragement. Share your experiences with trusted friends or family members.

Benefit: A supportive network provides a safety net during challenging times and reinforces positive changes.

The relentless pursuit of perfection can lead to severe psychological stress, including anxiety, depression, and erosion of self-esteem and confidence. Recognizing the signs of regressive perfectionism and taking proactive steps to manage it can help mitigate its detrimental effects. By embracing imperfection, setting realistic expectations, practicing self-compassion, and seeking support, individuals can foster a healthier mindset and improve their mental well-being. Understanding these impacts through lived experiences highlights the importance of addressing perfectionistic tendencies and cultivating a more balanced and fulfilling approach to life.

Paralysis by Analysis:

Regressive perfectionism often results in what is known as "paralysis by analysis." Individuals caught in this cycle overthink and overanalyze every decision and action, seeking to ensure perfection at every turn. This excessive scrutiny can be debilitating, preventing them from making any meaningful progress. They become consumed by the fear of making the wrong choice or not achieving a flawless outcome, leading to a state of inaction. For example, an artist might spend years perfecting a single piece, never feeling it is good enough to share with the world, thereby stalling their career.

Missed Opportunities:

By fixating on perfection, individuals frequently miss valuable opportunities for growth and development. The fear of failure or making mistakes causes them to avoid taking on new challenges or pursuing ambitious goals. This avoidance behavior limits their experiences and stifles their potential, leading to a life filled with unfulfilled dreams and aspirations.

For instance, consider a talented musician who continually delays releasing their music because it doesn't meet their impossibly high standards. While they endlessly tweak and perfect their songs, other musicians, with less hesitation, release their work, gain experience, and build an audience. The perfectionist musician, meanwhile, remains in the shadows, their talent unrecognized, their dreams unfulfilled.

Creative Minds at Risk:

Many creative minds have fallen victim to regressive perfectionism. Writers, artists, and innovators often abandon promising projects because they cannot achieve their ideal vision immediately. This is especially common in fields that rely heavily on subjective evaluation and personal expression. For instance, a writer might endlessly revise their manuscript, never feeling satisfied enough to submit it for publication. This pursuit of an unattainable perfect draft can prevent the writer from sharing their voice and stories with the world.

Consider the story of Franz Kafka, one of the most influential writers of the 20th century. Kafka was known for his perfectionist tendencies, which led him to request that his unfinished works be destroyed upon his death. Thankfully, his friend Max Brod ignored this request, and Kafka's works were published posthumously. Despite Kafka's perfectionism, his unfinished and unpolished manuscripts have had a profound impact on literature, illustrating that even imperfect work can be powerful and influential.

The Challenges George Washington Carver Overcame:

George Washington Carver, a pioneering Black inventor and agricultural scientist, epitomized the principle of progression over perfection. His journey was fraught with significant challenges and setbacks, yet his relentless pursuit of improvement led to groundbreaking advancements in agricultural science.

Early Life and Education:

Carver was born into slavery in Missouri during the Civil War. His early life was marked by adversity; he was orphaned as an infant when his mother was kidnapped by raiders. Raised by his former owners, Carver showed an early interest in plants and learning. Despite limited access to formal education due to racial discrimination, he pursued knowledge with tenacity. Carver's determination led him to seek education at a time when opportunities for Black Americans were severely restricted. He walked 10 miles to attend a school for Black children and later pursued higher education at Iowa

State Agricultural College, becoming the first Black student and faculty member there.

Racial Discrimination and Professional Struggles:

Throughout his career, Carver faced pervasive racial discrimination. As a Black scientist in a predominantly white society, he had to constantly prove his worth and fight for recognition. Despite his significant contributions, Carver often worked with limited resources and faced skepticism from peers. Nevertheless, he persevered, driven by a passion for science and a desire to help poor farmers improve their livelihoods.

Scientific Challenges and Breakthroughs:

Carver's work in agricultural science involved extensive experimentation and innovation. He developed crop rotation methods to restore nitrogen to depleted soils, promoting sustainable farming practices. Additionally, Carver advocated for the cultivation of alternative crops like peanuts and sweet potatoes, which provided nutritional and economic benefits to impoverished farmers in the South.

Carver's journey was marked by countless experiments, many of which failed. However, he viewed these failures as opportunities to learn and improve. His ability to embrace setbacks and continue making progress exemplified the principle of progression over perfection. Carver's ground-breaking contributions transformed agriculture, improved soil health, and provided economic opportunities for marginalized communities.

Understanding Progression:

Progression is about continuous growth and improvement. It acknowledges that perfection is an unattainable ideal and instead focuses on making progress towards our goals, one step at a time. By embracing progression, we free ourselves from the shackles of perfectionism and open ourselves up to new possibilities and experiences.

George Washington Carver epitomized this mindset. Despite facing numerous challenges and setbacks, Carver's relentless pursuit of improvement led to significant advancements in agricultural science. His work not only improved soil health but also provided economic opportunities for poor farmers in the South. Carver's ability to focus on incremental progress, rather than unattainable perfection, allowed him to make lasting contributions that continue to benefit society today.

Cultivating a Mindset of Progression:

Shifting from a perfectionist mindset to a progression-oriented mindset requires intentional effort and self-awareness. It involves letting go of unrealistic expectations and learning to embrace imperfection. One way to cultivate a mindset of progression is to set realistic goals and celebrate small victories along the way. By re-framing setbacks as opportunities for growth, we can overcome obstacles and continue moving forward.

The biblical story of Moses provides a powerful example of this. Initially reluctant and doubting his abilities, Moses faced numerous challenges and failures as he led the Israelites out of Egypt. Despite his speech impediment and initial reluctance to accept his role, Moses embraced his imperfections and focused on the progression of his mission. His unwavering commitment to progress, guided by faith and perseverance, eventually led to the liberation of his people and the delivery of the Ten Commandments.

Moses Overcoming His Speech Impediment:

Moses is one of the most significant figures in biblical history, known for leading the Israelites out of Egyptian captivity. However, his journey was not without its challenges. Moses had a speech impediment, which he initially saw as a significant barrier to his ability to lead. When God called Moses to free the Israelites, Moses expressed doubt about his capability due to his difficulty in speaking. Despite this, he accepted the role with the support of his brother Aaron, who helped him communicate his messages. Moses' story exemplifies how embracing one's imperfections and focusing on progression can lead to extraordinary achievements. His leadership and persistence in the face of personal and external obstacles illustrate the power of forward movement and the impact it can have on one's mission and legacy.

The Power of Forward Movement:

Forward movement is the engine that drives progress. It's about taking consistent action towards our goals, even in the face of uncertainty or setbacks. When we prioritize forward movement, we create momentum that propels us towards success. Each step we take brings us closer to realizing our dreams and aspirations.

George Washington Carver's career was marked by persistent forward movement. He didn't wait for perfect conditions or guaranteed success; instead, he continued to experiment, innovate, and educate others, gradually building a legacy that still influences agriculture today.

Embracing Imperfection and Finding Expression:

Our imperfections are what make us unique, and it's through embracing them that we find true expression. When we let go of the need to be perfect and instead focus on being authentic, we give ourselves permission to shine. By honoring our gifts and sharing them with the world, we not only enrich our own lives but also inspire others to do the same. Carver's work in agricultural science was not about achieving personal perfection but about making a meaningful impact. His willingness to embrace challenges and learn from failures allowed him to develop innovative solutions that had a lasting positive effect on society.

Conclusion:

In our journey towards personal and professional fulfillment, embracing progression over perfection is essential. It allows us to break free from the limitations of perfectionism and unleash our full potential. By prioritizing forward movement, embracing imperfection, and finding expression, we can create a life filled with purpose, joy, and meaning. Let the examples of George Washington Carver and Moses inspire you to pursue progress with determination and faith, knowing that each step forward brings you closer to realizing your potential and making a difference in the world.

Key Takeaways from the Chapter:
Embracing Progression Over Perfection:

1. Progression vs. Perfection:

Embracing progression over perfection unlocks true potential and leads to fulfillment and expression.

Progression focuses on continuous growth and improvement, acknowledging that perfection is unattainable.

2. Pitfalls of Regressive Perfectionism:

Regressive perfectionism leads to psychological stress, anxiety, depression, and eroded self-esteem.

This mindset causes paralysis by analysis, missed opportunities, and a cycle of inaction and regret.

Creative minds often abandon projects due to unattainable standards, stifling their potential.

3. George Washington Carver's Journey:

Carver overcame significant challenges, including racial discrimination and limited resources. His relentless pursuit of improvement led to advancements in agricultural science, benefiting marginalized communities. Carver's focus on incremental progress rather than perfection resulted in lasting contributions.

4. Moses' Leadership Despite Imperfections:

Moses overcame his speech impediment and initial reluctance to lead the Israelites out of captivity. His story exemplifies how embracing imperfections and focusing on progression can lead to extraordinary achievements.

5. Understanding and Cultivating a Mindset of Progression:

Shifting from a perfectionist to a progression-oriented mindset requires self-awareness and effort.

Setting realistic goals and celebrating small victories are crucial for embracing progression.

Reframing setbacks as growth opportunities help overcome obstacles.

6. Power of Forward Movement:

Consistent action towards goals, despite uncertainty or setbacks, creates momentum and propels towards success.

Forward movement drives progress and helps realize dreams and aspirations.

7. Embracing Imperfection and Finding Expression:

Imperfections make us unique, and embracing them allows for authentic self-expression. Focusing on authenticity rather than perfection enriches our lives and inspires others.

Conclusion:

Embracing progression over perfection breaks the limitations of perfectionism and unleashes its full potential. Prioritizing forward movement, embracing imperfection, and finding expression create a life filled with purpose, joy, and meaning. The examples of George Washington Carver and Moses inspire pursuing progress with determination and faith.

Chapter 12

My Journey from Darkness to Light: Cultivating Greatness

"It's in the darkness of the cocoon that greatness emerges. Greatness is not discovered in the spotlight; it is first developed in the darkness before it's revealed in the light."

C R Wallace

In this chapter, I reflect on my personal journey, intertwining it with biblical principles and examples to illuminate the transformative process of personal growth and the emergence of greatness. The metaphor of the cocoon serves as a poignant symbol for the development of one's potential and the journey from obscurity to prominence.

The Cocoon: A Metaphor for Transformation:

The cocoon, a seemingly insignificant and often overlooked part of nature, embodies the essence of transformation. Within this humble and concealed space, a caterpillar undergoes a profound metamorphosis, eventually emerging as a butterfly. This metamorphosis is not instantaneous but requires time, patience, and a series of internal changes. Similarly, personal growth and the emergence of greatness are processes that often occur away from the public eye, requiring a period of obscurity, introspection, and internal development.

The Cocoon: Nature's Hidden Workshop:

At first glance, the cocoon appears to be nothing more than a small, lifeless package suspended from a branch or hidden among leaves. However, this simple exterior belies the incredible transformation taking place inside. The caterpillar, having woven its cocoon, enters a state known as pupation. During this time, it breaks down its old body structures and forms new ones. Enzymes dissolve the caterpillar's tissues, turning it into a rich soup of cells that will reorganize and differentiate to form the organs, wings, and body parts of the adult butterfly.

This process, known as metamorphosis, is a remarkable feat of nature, demonstrating that significant change often happens out of sight, in a quiet and protected environment. The cocoon provides the caterpillar with safety and isolation, shielding it from external threats while it undergoes its radical transformation. This period of seclusion is crucial, as any premature exposure could disrupt the delicate process and prevent the emergence of a fully formed butterfly.

The Parallel of Personal Growth:

Personal growth mirrors this natural process in many ways.

Just as the caterpillar must retreat into its cocoon to transform, individuals often need to withdraw from their usual environments to foster their development. This retreat is not about physical seclusion alone but involves emotional and mental introspection. It is during these periods of introspection that individuals can reassess their goals, values, and identity.

The Importance of Time and Patience:

One of the most critical aspects of both the caterpillar's transformation and personal growth is the element of time. Just as the caterpillar cannot rush its metamorphosis, personal development cannot be hurried. It requires patience and an understanding that significant changes often occur gradually. In a world that prizes quick results and instant gratification, this can be a challenging lesson. However, the profound and lasting changes that define true personal growth necessitate a commitment to the process, much like the patient waiting within the cocoon.

Internal Changes:

During the cocoon phase, the caterpillar's internal structures are completely reconfigured. Similarly, personal growth often involves deep internal changes that are not immediately visible to others. This might include developing new skills, fostering emotional resilience, or gaining new perspectives. These changes are foundational and must occur before any external manifestations of growth and greatness can be observed.

The Period of Obscurity:

Significant personal growth often takes place in periods of obscurity. These are the times when an individual might feel hidden away from the world, working diligently and quietly on their self-improvement. It is in these moments of solitude and focus that true transformation occurs.

Embracing Introspection:

Introspection is a key component of this process. Taking time to reflect on past experiences, understanding personal strengths and weaknesses, and setting future goals are all critical to personal development. This self-examination allows for the shedding of old, limiting beliefs and the adoption of new, empowering ones.

Developing in Solitude:

Much like the caterpillar's transformation within the cocoon, personal growth often requires a level of solitude. This does not necessarily mean physical isolation but rather a focused withdrawal from distractions and external validations. This solitude provides the space needed to develop new ideas, cultivate creativity, and foster a deeper understanding of oneself.

The Emergence of Greatness:

Just as the caterpillar eventually emerges from the cocoon as a butterfly, individuals who undergo this process of internal transformation can step into their greatness. The butterfly's emergence is a powerful symbol of the potential that lies within each of us, waiting to be realized through dedication and introspection.

From Obscurity to Visibility:

When the transformation is complete, the once-hidden individual is ready to re-enter the world, now equipped with new strengths and insights. This emergence is not just about personal achievement but also about contributing to the broader community. The butterfly, now capable of flight, plays a vital role in pollination and the ecosystem, much like how individuals can impact and inspire those around them with their newfound capabilities.

The Cycle Continues:

The journey from obscurity to prominence is cyclical. Even after emerging, the process of growth and transformation continues. Each new phase of life may require another period of introspection and internal development, reminding us that personal growth is an ongoing journey rather than a final destination.

Conclusion:

The metaphor of the cocoon serves as a poignant reminder of the hidden and gradual nature of transformation. Both in nature and in personal growth, significant change requires time, patience, and a willingness to undergo profound internal changes away from the public eye. By embracing these periods of obscurity and introspection, individuals can develop their potential and ultimately emerge transformed, ready to achieve greatness and contribute meaningfully to the world.

Biblical Foundations of Transformation:

The Bible offers numerous examples of individuals who underwent significant transformations, reflecting the journey from potential to prominence. These stories provide timeless lessons and inspiration for our own personal growth journeys.

Moses: From Fugitive to Leader:

Moses' life illustrates a dramatic transformation. Initially, a fugitive fleeing from Egypt after killing an Egyptian, Moses spent 40 years in the wilderness as a shepherd. This period of obscurity served as his cocoon, where he developed the humility, patience, and resilience necessary for his future role. When God called upon him from the burning bush, Moses was ready to lead the Israelites out of bondage. His transformation from a fugitive to a leader of a nation underscores the importance of the cocoon phase in developing one's potential.

The Early Life of Moses: From Privilege to Exile:

Moses was born into a Hebrew family during a time when the Israelites were enslaved in Egypt. Rescued from a decree that all Hebrew male infants be killed, Moses was adopted by Pharaoh's daughter and raised in the Egyptian court, enjoying a life of privilege and education. However, aware of his Hebrew roots, Moses was troubled by the suffering of his people. His sense of justice and identity led him to intervene when he saw an Egyptian beating a Hebrew slave, resulting in the Egyptian's death. Fearing for his life, Moses fled to the land of Midian.

The Wilderness: Moses' Cocoon:

In Midian, Moses' life took a stark turn. From the opulence of Pharaoh's palace, he transitioned to the humble and rugged life of a shepherd. This 40-year period in the wilderness was his cocoon phase—a time of profound personal transformation away from the limelight and pressures of his former life.

Developing Humility:

Raised as a prince in Egypt, Moses had experienced power and privilege. However, tending sheep in the wilderness required humility. He had to adapt to a life of service, caring for the flock, and living in harmony with nature. This shift from ruling to serving was essential in shaping the humble leader Moses would become.

Cultivating Patience:

Shepherding is a slow, meticulous task that requires patience and perseverance. Moses learned to be patient with the unpredictable nature of his new environment and the animals he tended. This patience was crucial for his later role, as he would need to lead the Israelites through their own extended period of wandering in the desert.

Building Resilience:

The harsh conditions of the wilderness tested Moses' physical and mental resilience. He had to cope with the elements, protect his flock from predators, and navigate the challenges of a nomadic life. These experiences built a robust character, preparing him to face the formidable task of confronting Pharaoh and leading a nation to freedom.

The Burning Bush: A Call to Leadership:

Moses' transformation culminated in the divine encounter at the burning bush. God's call to Moses from within the flames was a pivotal moment, marking the transition from his cocoon phase to his emergence as a leader. By this time, Moses had developed the qualities needed for his mission—humility to serve God's purpose, patience to guide a rebellious people, and resilience to withstand the trials ahead.

Leading the Israelites: From Liberation to Legacy:

Empowered by his profound transformation, Moses returned to Egypt, armed with God's assurance and newfound strength. His leadership was characterized by the same qualities he had cultivated in the wilderness. He negotiated with Pharaoh, endured the plagues, and guided the Israelites out of slavery, through the Red Sea, and into the wilderness.

The Importance of the Cocoon Phase:

Moses' life underscores the importance of the cocoon phase in personal development. This period of seclusion and internal growth was crucial in preparing him for his monumental task. It highlights that significant transformation often requires stepping away from one's familiar environment and undergoing a period of profound change.

Lessons from Moses' Transformation:

1. **Humility in Leadership:**

True leadership requires humility. Moses learned to lead by serving others, a lesson forged in the quiet fields of Midian.

2. Patience in Process:

Personal and spiritual growth is a gradual process. Moses' 40 years as a shepherd taught him the patience necessary to lead a nation through decades of wandering.

3. Resilience in Adversity:

Adversity builds strength. The challenges Moses faced in the wilderness equipped him with the resilience to confront and overcome future obstacles.

Moses' journey from a fugitive to a national leader illustrates the transformative power of the cocoon phase. It is in these periods of obscurity and introspection that individuals can develop the essential qualities needed for their future roles. Moses' story encourages us to embrace our own cocoon phases, trusting that these times of hidden growth are preparing us for greater purposes ahead.

David: From Shepherd to King:

David's journey from shepherd boy to King of Israel is another powerful example. Anointed by the prophet Samuel while still tending sheep, David's path to kingship was fraught with challenges, including years of fleeing from King Saul. During this time, David honed his leadership skills, deepened his faith in God, and learned the intricacies of governance and warfare. His time in the metaphorical cocoon was essential for his emergence as a wise and just ruler.

Personal Reflections: Embracing the Cocoon:

In my own life, I have experienced periods of obscurity that, in retrospect, were critical for my personal growth. These phases were often marked by challenges, self-doubt, and a sense of being hidden away from the world. However, much like the caterpillar in its cocoon, these times were essential for my transformation.

Early Career Struggles:

During the early stages of my career, I faced numerous setbacks and periods of unemployment. These times felt like being in a cocoon, isolated and seemingly stagnant. However, these experiences forced me to develop resilience, creativity, and a deeper understanding of my purpose. I took this time to acquire new skills, seek mentorship, and reflect on my aspirations.

Spiritual Growth:

My spiritual journey also mirrored the cocoon metaphor. There were seasons when I felt distant from my faith and questioned my path. It was in these quiet, introspective moments that I turned to biblical teachings for guidance and inspiration. The stories of transformation in the Bible provided comfort and a roadmap for my own journey, reinforcing the idea that periods of obscurity are not wasted but are integral to personal growth.

The Emergence: From Obscurity to Prominence:

Emerging from the cocoon signifies the moment when internal transformations become visible to the outside world. It is the phase where one steps into their potential, ready to impact and inspire others.

Embracing Opportunities:

When opportunities finally presented themselves, I was prepared. The time spent in the cocoon had equipped me with the necessary skills, knowledge, and character to seize these moments. Just as a butterfly emerged ready to fly, I was ready to take on new challenges and responsibilities.

Impacting Others:

Emerging from the cocoon is not just about personal achievement but also about influencing and helping others. My journey taught me the importance of mentorship, community, and giving back. By sharing my experiences and the lessons learned during my transformation, I hope to inspire others to embrace their own cocoon phases and trust in the process of growth.

Conclusion:

The metaphor of the cocoon serves as a powerful reminder

that transformation is a gradual and often hidden process. By intertwining my personal journey with biblical principles, I have come to appreciate the significance of the cocoon phase in developing one's potential. This journey from obscurity to prominence is not only about achieving personal greatness but also about preparing to make a meaningful impact on the world. Embrace the cocoon, trust the process, and emerge transformed and ready to soar.

David's journey from shepherd boy to King of Israel is another powerful example. Anointed by the prophet Samuel while still tending sheep, David's path to kingship was fraught with challenges, including years of fleeing from King Saul. During this time, David honed his leadership skills, deepened his faith in God, and learned the intricacies of governance and warfare. His time in the metaphorical cocoon was essential for his emergence as a wise and just ruler.

Early Life: The Shepherd Boy:

David's early life was characterized by simplicity and humility. As the youngest son of Jesse, David was tasked with tending his father's sheep. This role might have seemed insignificant, but it was here that David began to develop qualities that would later define his leadership.

Developing Responsibility and Courage:

Shepherding was not an easy task. David had to protect his flock from predators, such as lions and bears, which required both courage and responsibility. These early experiences taught him to be vigilant, brave, and protective—traits that were crucial in his later battles and leadership roles.

Defeating Goliath: A Testament to Early Training

David's encounter with Goliath is one of the most iconic stories from his life, showcasing the profound impact of his early experiences as a shepherd. When faced with the giant Philistine warrior, David's confidence stemmed from his previous victories over predators like lions and bears. He drew on these experiences, using his skills with a sling to defeat Goliath, demonstrating that the courage and resourcefulness developed in his shepherding days were instrumental in his early public triumphs.

Anointing by Samuel:

David's life took a significant turn when the prophet Samuel visited his home to anoint the next king of Israel. Despite being the youngest and seemingly least likely choice among his brothers, David was chosen by God. This anointing marked the beginning of his journey towards kingship, but it also signaled the start of a period of trials and preparation.

The Wilderness Years: David's Cocoon:

After his anointing, David's path was far from straightforward. He entered a metaphorical cocoon phase characterized by years of hardship and exile. His time fleeing from King Saul, who saw David as a threat to his throne, was a period of significant personal growth and development.

Fleeing from Saul: A Test of Endurance:

David spent many years on the run, living in caves, forests, and foreign lands to escape Saul's relentless pursuit. This period tested his endurance and resilience. Constantly facing danger, David learned to trust in God's protection and guidance, deepening his faith and reliance on divine support.

Leadership in Exile:

Despite being a fugitive, David began to gather a group of followers—men who were discontented and in debt, seeking refuge with him. Leading this diverse and often desperate group, David honed his leadership skills. He learned to inspire loyalty, manage conflicts, and make strategic decisions, all while remaining under constant threat from Saul.

Moral and Ethical Challenges:

David's time in exile was also marked by significant moral and ethical challenges. On several occasions, he had the opportunity to kill Saul and seize the throne, but he chose to spare Saul's life, respecting God's anointed king. These decisions reflected David's commitment to righteousness and his understanding of justice and mercy—qualities that would later define his rule.

Learning Governance and Warfare:

David's experiences during his years of exile also provided him with invaluable lessons in governance and warfare. His interactions with various tribes and his role as a military leader helped him understand the complexities of ruling a diverse population and the intricacies of military strategy.

Building Alliances:

During his time on the run, David forged alliances with various groups and tribes, learning the importance of diplomacy and negotiation. These alliances were crucial in his eventual consolidation of power and unification of Israel.

Mastering Warfare:

Leading his men in various skirmishes and battles, David developed a keen understanding of military tactics and strategy. His successes in these endeavors built his reputation as a formidable warrior and leader, earning him the loyalty and respect of his followers.

Emergence as King: From Shepherd to Sovereign:

After Saul's death, David's journey to kingship came to fruition. Initially ruling over Judah, David eventually united all the tribes of Israel, establishing Jerusalem as the political and spiritual center of the nation. His emergence as king was marked by the qualities he had developed during his cocoon phase—humility, resilience, faith, and a deep understanding of leadership.

A Wise and Just Ruler:

David's reign was characterized by justice, wisdom, and a deep commitment to God. He sought to rule not with an iron fist, but with fairness and compassion, always mindful of the lessons learned during his years of hardship.

Deepening His Faith:

David's psalms and prayers reflect a profound relationship with God, shaped by his experiences in the wilderness. His faith was central to his kingship, guiding his decisions and policies. This spiritual depth was a source of strength for both David and the nation of Israel.

Legacy of Leadership:

David's legacy as a ruler extends beyond his military victories and political achievements. His life story, marked by transformation and growth, serves as a timeless example of how adversity and obscurity can prepare an individual for greatness. His journey from shepherd boy to king underscores the importance of the cocoon phase in developing one's potential and character.

David's journey from a shepherd boy to the King of Israel illustrates the transformative power of the cocoon phase. His years of obscurity, filled with challenges and growth opportunities, were essential in shaping him into a wise and just ruler. David's story reminds us that personal growth often requires enduring trials and embracing periods of seclusion, during which our character and abilities are honed. By trusting in the process and remaining faithful, we can emerge from our own cocoons ready to fulfill our potential and make a meaningful impact.

The biblical principle that rewards are bestowed openly for deeds done in secret resonates deeply with me. This idea reinforces the importance of investing in personal growth and development, even when it may go unnoticed by others.

Throughout my journey, I have learned the value of patience and organic growth. Rushing the process of personal development can lead to detrimental outcomes, much like the risks associated with premature childbirth. It is essential to allow oneself the time and space needed to mature and develop fully before seeking or accepting significant responsibilities.

I have witnessed firsthand the consequences of entrusting important roles to individuals who lack the necessary experience and maturity. This is akin to handing over the keys to a luxury car to a child – chaos and harm are inevitable. Therefore, it is crucial to prioritize personal growth and development before seeking or granting promotions.

Drawing from biblical teachings, I understand the importance of avoiding the appointment of novices. Such individuals are prone to pride and downfall, as they may lack the humility and wisdom needed to navigate their responsibilities effectively.

Ultimately, my journey has taught me the virtues of patience and perseverance. By embracing these qualities, I have been able to navigate the journey from darkness to light with wisdom and grace. I believe that by investing in personal growth and development, we can all cultivate greatness and realize our fullest potential.

The biblical principle that rewards are bestowed openly for deeds done in secret resonates deeply with me. This idea underscores the importance of investing in personal growth and development, even when it may go unnoticed by others.

The Principle of Hidden Growth:

The notion that true rewards come from efforts made in secret speaks to the essence of genuine personal development. In a world that often prizes visible achievements and immediate recognition, this principle reminds us that the most significant transformations occur away from the spotlight. It encourages a focus on internal growth, character building, and the nurturing of one's abilities and virtues in private.

Learning Patience and Embracing Organic Growth:

Throughout my journey, I have learned the value of patience and organic growth. Personal development is a process that cannot be rushed. Much like the risks associated with premature childbirth, hastening the maturation process can lead to detrimental outcomes. Each stage of growth serves a purpose, providing essential lessons and experiences that contribute to overall maturity and readiness for future responsibilities.

The Dangers of Premature Advancement:

Rushing personal growth is akin to pushing a seedling to bloom before it has established strong roots. Without a solid foundation, any progress made is precarious and likely to collapse under pressure. This is a vital lesson in understanding that true readiness for significant roles and responsibilities comes only with time, experience, and deliberate growth.

The Consequences of Premature Responsibility:

I have witnessed firsthand the consequences of entrusting important roles to individuals who lack the necessary experience and maturity. This is akin to handing over the keys to a luxury car to a child – chaos and harm are inevitable. When unprepared individuals are placed in positions of power or responsibility, the results can be disastrous for both the individuals and the entities they serve.

Biblical Teachings on the Importance of Maturity:

Drawing from biblical teachings, I understand the importance of avoiding the appointment of novices to positions of authority. The Bible cautions against this in 1 Timothy 3:6, which warns that a novice may become conceited and fall into the condemnation of the devil. Novices are prone to pride and downfall because they may lack the humility and wisdom needed to navigate their responsibilities effectively. This wisdom underscores the necessity of allowing individuals the time and experience to develop fully before assuming significant roles.

The Virtues of Patience and Perseverance:

Ultimately, my journey has taught me the virtues of patience and perseverance. By embracing these qualities, I have been able to navigate the journey from darkness to light with wisdom and grace.

The process of personal growth is often challenging and requires enduring periods of obscurity and struggle. However, these phases are crucial for developing resilience, character, and true capability.

Investing in Personal Growth:

By investing in personal growth and development, we cultivate the foundation for lasting success and greatness. This investment involves:

1. **Commitment to Continuous Learning****:

Engaging in lifelong learning and seeking knowledge and wisdom from various sources, including mentors, experiences, and self-reflection.

2. **Embracing Challenges:**

Viewing obstacles and setbacks as opportunities for growth and learning rather than as insurmountable barriers.

3. **Fostering Humility:**

Maintaining a humble attitude, recognizing that there is always more to learn and room for improvement.

4. **Practicing Patience:**

Understanding that true growth takes time and that rushing the process can lead to incomplete development and potential failure.

My journey has reinforced the importance of hidden growth,

patience, and the dangers of premature responsibility. By adhering to the principle that rewards come from deeds done in secret and investing in personal growth, we can cultivate the virtues needed to navigate life's challenges with wisdom and grace. Embracing patience and perseverance allows us to realize our fullest potential, ultimately achieving greatness not just for ourselves but for those we lead and influence. Through deliberate and mindful personal development, we prepare ourselves to handle significant responsibilities with the maturity and wisdom they require.

Summary:

In the chapter "My Journey from Darkness to Light: Cultivating Greatness," the author reflects on the transformative process of personal growth, drawing parallels between their journey and biblical principles. Using the metaphor of the cocoon, the chapter illustrates how greatness often develops in obscurity before being revealed in the light. The cocoon represents a period of introspection, patience, and internal change, akin to the biblical transformations of Moses and David. These periods of seclusion and hidden growth are crucial for developing the resilience, humility, and wisdom necessary for future responsibilities. The chapter emphasizes the importance of embracing these phases, trusting that they prepare individuals for their eventual emergence into prominence and ability to impact the world positively.

Key Points from the chapter: 

1. Metaphor of the Cocoon:

Symbolizes the hidden process of personal transformation. Represents the necessary period of introspection and internal development before achieving greatness.

2. The Cocoon in Nature:

Describes the metamorphosis of a caterpillar into a butterfly. Highlights the importance of time, patience, and protection during this transformative phase.

3. Parallel to Personal Growth:

Personal growth requires periods of retreat and introspection.

Emphasizes the necessity of patience and gradual development.

4. Importance of Time and Patience:

Personal development cannot be rushed. True and lasting changes require a commitment to the process.

5. Internal Changes:

Personal growth involves deep internal transformations, such as developing new skills and emotional resilience.

These changes are foundational and precede external manifestations of greatness.

6. Period of Obscurity:

Significant personal growth often occurs in times of obscurity and seclusion.

These moments allow for focused self-improvement and transformation.

7. Biblical Foundations of Transformation:

Uses the stories of Moses and David to illustrate the cocoon metaphor.

Moses' transformation from a fugitive to a leader during his 40 years in the wilderness.

David's journey from shepherd to king is characterized by years of challenges and growth.

8. Lessons from Moses' and David's Transformations:

Humility, patience, and resilience are critical qualities developed during periods of obscurity.

These biblical figures emerged from their cocoons, ready to lead and impact others.

9. Personal Reflections:

The author shares their own experiences of growth during periods of challenge and seclusion.

Emphasizes the importance of these phases in developing resilience and creativity.

10. Emergence of Greatness:

The transition from obscurity to prominence signifies readiness to impact and inspire others.

Personal growth is not only about individual achievement but also about contributing to the broader community.

11. Ongoing Nature of Growth:

Personal development is a continuous journey with repeated cycles of introspection and transformation.

Each phase prepares individuals for greater purposes ahead.

Chapter 13

Visionary Triumph: The Vital Role of Destiny Helpers

Destiny helpers are God's agents of support, assisting visionaries with the determination to see their visions through to fruition.

C R Wallace

In this chapter, I would like to introduce Jake Ellis Kuria. Jake Ellis Kuria, a refugee from Kenya, became a divine agent supporting the vision given to me by God: reaching the world through my podcast, YouTube channel, social media platform, and books.

The journey began when I attended an orientation meeting

at Brampton City Hall for refugees who had recently arrived in Canada from Africa.

Despite the cold November day in 2023 and a long day of work, I felt a strong prompt to attend the orientation. I've always believed obedience is better than sacrifice.

At the end of the orientation, refugees were asked about their skills and experiences that could benefit the community and generate income for them. Jake mentioned he was a tattoo artist. After hearing this, I sought him out, and we exchanged phone numbers.

This seemingly insignificant encounter turned out to be significant and divine. In January 2023, following a spiritual prompting, I got my first tattoo, a figure 8 with a cross, symbolizing infinity and new beginnings, despite ridicule from religious individuals.

This experience taught me that on the path to fulfilling your preordained destiny, individuals who never offered advice may become unsolicited advisors. Regardless, remain steadfast in your convictions.

Jake and I didn't end up doing tattoos together. Instead, we launched the podcast "Icons Talk," built a website, co-designed a book cover, and collaborated on various projects.

Meeting Jake was significant. If I hadn't gotten that first tattoo, we might not have connected. His support has been instrumental in fulfilling my destiny.

Jake noticed quotes I posted on my WhatsApp status and expressed a desire to add his touch to them. We met at a restaurant, discussed our vision, and decided to work together, setting clear goals and timelines.

The actual conversation text I had from Jake regarding him working with me on my post was, "Let me add some sauce to your post."

His Jake sauce is now more famous to me than Jamaican jerk sauce.

After our initial meeting, Jake and I reconvened to outline our strategy for moving forward with the project. In this follow-up meeting, we decided to apply the SMART principles, Specific, Measurable, Achievable, Relevant, and Time-bound—to ensure our goals were clearly defined and attainable.

We began by setting specific objectives for each phase of the project. Instead of vague goals, we identified precise tasks, such as creating content outlines, recording videos, editing, and promoting our channel. This specificity helped us understand exactly what needed to be done and prevented any ambiguity.

Next, we established methods to make our goals measurable. To track our progress effectively, we decided to utilize the analytics tools available on our platform. We monitored key metrics such as the number of subscribers, video views, watch time, and audience engagement. By logging these figures weekly, we could visualize our growth, identify trends, and adjust our strategy as needed.

Ensuring our goals were achievable was a crucial step. We assessed our current skillsets, resources, and time availability. Jake's experience with video editing was a significant advantage, allowing us to produce high-quality content more efficiently. We also planned to leverage online tutorials and software tools to enhance our capabilities in areas where we needed improvement. This realistic approach helped us avoid setting ourselves up for failure by aiming too high too soon.

Our goals were also relevant to our overarching mission. We wanted to create valuable content that resonated with our target audience and aligned with our channel's purpose. Each goal was designed to contribute directly to this mission, ensuring our efforts remained focused and meaningful.

Finally, we defined deadlines for each task. By setting specific timelines, such as a one-week deadline for scripting a video or a two-week period for completing the editing of multiple videos, we created a sense of urgency and maintained momentum. These deadlines also allowed us to plan and prioritize our workload effectively.

By applying the SMART principles and leveraging platform

analytics, we transformed our initial ideas into a structured, actionable plan, increasing our chances of success and enabling us to track our progress systematically.

There's an aspect of my encounter with Jake that I haven't emphasized yet. When we met, he didn't mention his skills in digital content production. He only mentioned being a tattoo artist. This encounter underscores the importance of seizing opportunities, even when they don't seem obvious.

If I hadn't gotten that first tattoo, Jake and I might not have connected, and my vision might not have been realized. I hope sharing this experience inspires you to stay focused on your goals despite others' opinions.

Destiny helpers are an integral part of our life's journey, manifesting in various forms, each with its unique impact on our growth and purpose. Supporters, like Jake, provide invaluable encouragement, guidance, and assistance as we navigate our paths. They offer unwavering support, lending a helping hand whenever needed and cheering us on during both triumphs and challenges.

On the other hand, betrayers, like Judas, present a different yet equally significant role in shaping our destinies. While their actions may be painful and disruptive, they challenge us to reassess our beliefs, values, and goals. Betrayers force us to confront adversity head-on, teaching us valuable lessons about trust, discernment, and resilience. In their betrayal, we find opportunities for self-reflection and personal growth, ultimately leading us closer to our true purpose.

Whether they appear as allies or adversaries, destiny helpers play a vital role in shaping our narratives. Their presence, whether supportive or challenging, serves as a catalyst for transformation, pushing us to evolve, adapt, and fulfill our destinies. Embracing the contributions of both supporters and betrayers enables us to navigate life's twists and turns with grace, gratitude, and a deeper understanding of ourselves and our purpose.

During this period, I found myself engulfed in a toxic work environment that eventually culminated in my wrongful dismissal. Initially, the experience was disheartening and distressing. However, as time passed, I began to recognize that what initially seemed like a setback was, in fact, a catalyst for profound transformation and newfound opportunities.

The timing of my wrongful dismissal proved to be a pivotal moment in my life, providing me with the necessary space and freedom to pursue endeavors that had long been lingering in the depths of my mind. Freed from the constraints of the toxic workplace, I found myself with the time, energy, and motivation to delve into new ventures that had previously seemed out of reach.

One of the most significant ventures that emerged from this

period of upheaval was the creation of my own channel, podcast, and this book. With the newfound freedom to explore my passions and interests, I dedicated myself wholeheartedly to these creative endeavors. I poured my energy into crafting engaging content for my channel, recording thought-provoking episodes for my podcast, and penning the pages of my book.

The timing of my dismissal allowed me to channel my experiences and emotions into these projects, infusing them with authenticity, depth, and meaning. Rather than allowing myself to be consumed by bitterness or resentment, I used my creative pursuits as a means of catharsis and self-expression. Through my channel, podcast, and book, I found a platform to share my story, connect with others who may be facing similar challenges, and inspire hope and resilience in the face of adversity.

In hindsight, I realize that what initially felt like a devastating blow was, in reality, a blessing in disguise. My wrongful dismissal forced me to confront my circumstances head-on, empowering me to reclaim my narrative, pursue my passions, and forge a path that aligned more closely with my values and aspirations. It served as a potent reminder that sometimes, out of the darkest moments, the brightest opportunities can emerge.

With God's guidance, Jake and I achieved more in a month than many do in a lifetime. As I write this, it's been less than two months since I met Jake, and I'm about to release this book on August 24, 2024. How great is our God?

Life's challenges can be turned into opportunities to fulfill your purpose and positively impact others.

Never give up on your dreams.

Metaphorically speaking, we can use the bitter lemons of life along with the sweetness of its sugar to create lemonade that not only refreshes us but also others, akin to a cold drink on a hot summer day.

Jake Ellis Kuria emerged as a divine agent, intricately woven into the fabric of my journey towards realizing my vision. From a chance encounter at a refugee orientation to becoming a pivotal collaborator in my endeavors, Jake's presence has been nothing short of providential.

Our initial connection, sparked by a shared passion for creativity and a willingness to explore uncharted territories, blossomed into a partnership that transcended conventional boundaries. Despite starting with the art of tattooing, Jake's role evolved into something far more profound—a catalyst for manifesting destiny.

As we embarked on our collaborative projects, navigating through challenges and celebrating triumphs, Jake's unwavering support and innovative contributions illuminated the path towards fulfillment. His "Jake sauce" infused each endeavor with a unique flavor, enriching our shared vision and amplifying its impact.

Our journey together exemplifies the serendipitous nature of destiny helpers, individuals whose presence in our lives, whether anticipated or unexpected, propels us towards our divine purpose. Jake's transition from a tattoo artist to a digital content collaborator underscores the importance of seizing opportunities, even when they appear disguised in unconventional forms.

Amidst life's adversities, including a toxic work environment and wrongful dismissal, Jake and I harnessed the transformative power of resilience and creativity. With God's guidance as our compass, we defied the odds and achieved milestones that surpassed even our wildest expectations.

As I reflect on our journey, culminating in the forthcoming release of this book, I am reminded of the profound truth that life's challenges can indeed be transformed into opportunities for growth and impact. Through perseverance, faith, and the support of destiny helpers like Jake, we can turn the bitter lemons of adversity into the sweet nectar of purpose.

As this chapter closes, I extend my deepest gratitude to Jake Ellis Kuria and all the destiny helpers who have illuminated my path. May our collective journey inspire others to embrace their dreams, navigate life's twists and turns with courage, and never lose sight of the transformative power of serendipity.

Key Points: from the chapter Visionary Triumph: The Vital Role of Destiny Helpers:

1. Introduction to Jake Ellis Kuria, a refugee from Kenya, who became a divine agent supporting the vision to reach the world through various platforms.

2. The journey began at an orientation meeting for refugees in Canada, where Jake's mention of being a tattoo artist sparked a connection.

3. Despite initial ridicule for getting a tattoo, the experience taught the importance of staying steadfast in convictions on the path to fulfilling destiny.

4. Jake and the author collaborated on launching the podcast "Icons Talk," website building, book cover design, and various projects.

5. The application of SMART principles to set clear goals and timelines for the project.

6. Emphasis on seizing opportunities, even when they seem unconventional.

7. Recognition of destiny helpers, who can take various forms, including both supportive and challenging roles.

8. Experience of overcoming a toxic work environment and turning challenges into opportunities for growth.

9. Achieving significant progress with Jake in a short time frame, highlighting the impact of divine guidance.

10. Encouragement to never give up on dreams and to use life's challenges to positively impact oneself and others.

11. Metaphorically, using life's bitter experiences along with its sweet moments to create something refreshing and impactful, akin to lemonade on a hot summer day.

Chapter 14
Navigating Relationships: The Art of Acceptance and Avoidance

"Never underestimate or overestimate anyone. When they reveal who they are, accept that's who they are and learn to navigate around them or avoid them. It takes too much energy to attempt to change them into someone else. A snake is a snake; it can be toxic and venomous. Avoid them, akin to backstabbers who will stab you in the back, so avoid them.

My eldest sister taught me this analogy: 'Use the act of sleeping akin to death.'

Let me give you an example of this statement: If someone goes out of their way to gossip negatively about others, they will do the same to you. Don't entertain them. On the other hand, if someone regularly speaks positively about others, connect with them. They will uplift you, and you can likewise uplift them with positive energy."

C R Wallace

Understanding and Navigating Human Nature: Recognizing and Managing Toxic Individuals

In the journey of human connections, it is crucial to strike a balance between not underestimating and overestimating anyone.

People often reveal their true selves through their actions and behaviors. Accepting this reality allows you to navigate relationships more effectively, conserving your energy for positive interactions rather than futile attempts to change others. Recognizing and managing toxic individuals is essential for maintaining your emotional well-being and protecting yourself from harm.

The Reality of Human Nature

1. Acceptance of True Selves

Insight: People will inevitably show their true colors over time. When someone reveals who they are, it's important to believe them. This acceptance prevents the disappointment and frustration that comes from expecting someone to behave differently than they naturally do.

Lived Experience: Consider Emma, who constantly tried to change her friend Sarah's unreliable behavior. Despite Emma's efforts, Sarah continued to cancel plans last minute and broke promises. Once Emma accepted Sarah's true nature, she adjusted her expectations and avoided relying on Sarah for important commitments, reducing her own stress and disappointment.

2. Energy Conservation

Insight: Attempting to change someone into a different person requires immense energy and often leads to frustration. It is far more efficient to recognize people for who they are and navigate relationships accordingly.

Lived Experience: John spent years trying to get his partner to adopt a healthier lifestyle. His partner's resistance caused constant conflict and drained John's energy. When John stopped trying to force change and instead focused on his own well-being, he felt more at peace and less stressed.

Recognizing Toxic Individuals

1. Identifying Toxic Traits

Insight: Toxic individuals often exhibit consistent negative behaviors such as manipulation, dishonesty, and backstabbing. Recognizing these traits early on can help you avoid deeper involvement with such individuals.

Lived Experience: Lisa worked with a colleague, Tom, who frequently gossiped and undermined others to get ahead. Initially, Lisa tried to befriend Tom, hoping to change his behavior. Over time, she realized that Tom's actions were ingrained in his character. By distancing herself from him and focusing on her own work, Lisa protected herself from his toxic influence.

2. Understanding Manipulation

Insight: Manipulative individuals often disguise their true intentions and use others for their benefit. Recognizing manipulative tactics can help you avoid falling victim to them.

Lived Experience: Michael had a friend, Alex, who always seemed to have ulterior motives. Alex would only reach out when he needed something and would disappear when Michael needed support. Recognizing this pattern, Michael chose to set clear boundaries and limited his interactions with Alex, thereby reducing his own frustration and emotional strain.

Navigating and Avoiding Toxic Relationships

1. Setting Boundaries:

Strategy: Establish clear boundaries with individuals who exhibit toxic behaviors. Communicate your limits and stick to them firmly.

Benefit: Setting boundaries protects your emotional well-being and prevents toxic individuals from taking advantage of you.

Lived Experience: Sarah had a family member who constantly criticized and belittled her. By setting boundaries, such as limiting the frequency and duration of their interactions, Sarah was able to maintain her self-esteem and reduce stress.

2. Avoiding Backstabbers:

Strategy: Recognize the signs of backstabbing, such as gossiping, betrayal, and deceit, and take steps to distance yourself from such individuals.

Benefit: Avoiding backstabbers prevents emotional harm and maintains your integrity and trustworthiness.

Lived Experience: When Jake realized that his coworker, Rob, was spreading rumors about him to get ahead, he decided to avoid sharing personal information with Rob and focused on building alliances with trustworthy colleagues. This not only protected Jake's reputation but also fostered a more supportive work environment.

3. Navigating around Toxic Individuals:

Strategy: Learn to navigate around toxic individuals by minimizing interactions and focusing on positive relationships.

Benefit: This approach conserves your energy for productive and supportive relationships, enhancing your overall well-being.

Lived Experience: Emily worked in an office with a particularly negative and toxic team member, Karen. Instead of engaging in Karen's negativity, Emily chose to collaborate more with her supportive colleagues. This shift allowed Emily to stay motivated and maintain a positive work environment.

Conclusion

Recognizing and managing toxic individuals is crucial for maintaining your emotional well-being. By accepting people for who they are and learning to navigate around or avoid toxic behaviors, you can protect yourself from unnecessary stress and harm. Setting boundaries, understanding manipulation, and avoiding backstabbers are essential strategies for dealing with toxic relationships. Drawing from lived experiences, these insights highlight the importance of conserving your energy for positive interactions and fostering a supportive network of relationships.

Navigating relationships involves understanding and accepting people for who they are, while also being discerning about who to keep in your circle. In my own life, I once had a friend who constantly belittled others behind their backs. Initially, I tried to overlook this behavior, hoping it was just a phase. However, as time went on, I realized that this negativity was ingrained in their character. Accepting this reality, I chose to distance myself from them to protect my own peace of mind. This decision wasn't easy, but it was necessary for my well-being. It taught me the importance of setting boundaries and surrounding myself with individuals who uplift and support me, rather than drain my energy with toxic behavior.

On the other hand, I've had the pleasure of knowing individuals who radiate positivity and kindness. One such person always spoke highly of others, even in their absence. Connecting with them not only uplifted my spirits but also enriched my life with their positive energy. In return, I made a conscious effort to reciprocate this positivity, fostering a mutually uplifting relationship.

Their unwavering positivity served as a beacon of light during challenging times, reminding me of the power of kindness and compassion. Their genuine warmth and sincerity made every interaction a joyous experience, leaving a lasting impact on my outlook on life and relationships.

In essence, navigating relationships requires a delicate balance of acceptance and avoidance. Recognizing when to embrace someone's true nature and when to steer clear of toxic influences can greatly enhance our well-being and foster healthier connections. Just as my sister's analogy suggests, understanding the analogy of sleeping akin to death can serve as a guiding principle in discerning which relationships to nurture and which to let go of.

Embracing individuals who exude positivity and kindness while being discerning about those who spread negativity allows us to cultivate a supportive and uplifting social circle. By surrounding ourselves with people who inspire and encourage us, we create an environment conducive to personal growth, happiness, and fulfillment.

Navigating relationships is indeed a delicate dance between

acceptance and avoidance, a lesson I've learned through a myriad of life experiences. One significant revelation is to never underestimate or overestimate anyone. This realization crystallized through encounters that challenged my initial perceptions and assumptions.

Take, for instance, a colleague at work who initially exuded friendliness and support. Yet, as time unfurled, their demeanor morphed, revealing a tendency for gossip and office politics. Rather than futilely attempting to alter their behavior, I embraced the reality of who they were. Instead, I chose to circumvent their negativity, directing my focus towards my professional duties while steadfastly maintaining boundaries.

This encounter taught me the importance of discernment in relationships. While it's tempting to believe the best in everyone, it's equally vital to acknowledge and respond to behaviors that veer from our values. By recognizing and accepting the true nature of individuals, we empower ourselves to navigate relationships with clarity and integrity, safeguarding our well-being in the process.

Similarly, I've encountered individuals within social circles whose behaviors mirrored toxicity, manifesting as manipulation and deceit. Like the venom of a snake, their actions had the potential to inflict harm if not vigilantly avoided. Recognizing the danger posed by these negative influences, I made a deliberate choice to create distance between myself and such individuals.

This decision wasn't made lightly. It required a deep introspection and a commitment to prioritizing my well-being and emotional health above all else. While it's never easy to sever ties or create boundaries, especially with individuals we once considered friends, it's essential for our growth and self-preservation.

By acknowledging the toxicity in these relationships and taking proactive steps to disengage, I reclaimed agency over my life and surroundings. I cultivated a sense of empowerment, knowing that I had the autonomy to choose the company I kept and the influences I allowed into my sphere.

This experience underscored the importance of discernment and self-care in navigating relationships. It taught me that while it's natural to seek connection and camaraderie, it's equally crucial to safeguard ourselves against harmful influences. Just as we would avoid a snake's venomous bite, we must exercise caution in choosing the company we keep, prioritizing relationships that uplift and nourish our souls.

The analogy of using sleep akin to death, as taught by my eldest sister, also resonated deeply. It serves as a reminder to be discerning about the company we keep. For instance, if someone habitually speaks negatively about others, it's a red flag that they may do the same behind our backs. By not entertaining such behavior, we safeguard ourselves from unnecessary drama and toxicity.

Conversely, surrounding oneself with individuals who radiate positivity can have a profound impact. I vividly recall a friend whose presence was like a beacon of light in my life. Consistently, they uplifted others with their kind words, genuine empathy, and unwavering encouragement. Connecting with them felt like a breath of fresh air, infusing my days with renewed hope, inspiration, and support.

Our friendship wasn't just about laughter and good times; it was a transformative experience that transcended surface-level interactions. It was a reciprocal exchange of positive energy, where each encounter left us both feeling uplifted and empowered to tackle life's challenges with renewed vigor.

In essence, navigating relationships requires a delicate blend of acceptance and avoidance. By acknowledging people for who they truly are—both their strengths and limitations—and choosing our associations wisely, we cultivate healthier, more fulfilling connections that enrich our lives. It's about embracing those who uplift and inspire us while simultaneously setting boundaries with those whose energy drains us or leads us astray from our true path.

Through these experiences, we learn to navigate the intricate balance of human relationships with grace and discernment, fostering connections that nurture our souls and propel us towards growth and fulfillment.

In conclusion, navigating relationships is a journey that requires a nuanced understanding of acceptance and avoidance. It's about recognizing people for who they truly are and making informed choices about who to keep in our lives. Whether it's distancing ourselves from toxic influences or embracing uplifting connections, the key lies in finding a balance that fosters our well-being and enriches our lives.

As we navigate the complexities of human interaction, let us remember the wisdom imparted by the analogy of sleeping akin to death. Just as we choose our companions carefully in life, so too must we be discerning about the company we keep. By prioritizing authenticity, positivity, and mutual respect, we can cultivate relationships that nurture our growth and bring out the best in ourselves and others.

So, let us approach each relationship with clarity and intention, honoring both our boundaries and our capacity for connection. In doing so, we pave the way for deeper, more meaningful connections that enrich our lives and contribute to our overall well-being.

The Chapter's Key Points:

1. Acceptance and Avoidance:

It's essential to accept people for who they are and learn to navigate around or avoid them accordingly. Attempting to change someone into someone else is futile and drains energy.

2. Toxic Influences:

Just as a snake's venom can be harmful, toxic individuals can cause harm if not avoided. Recognizing toxic behaviors and distancing oneself from such influences is crucial for emotional well-being.

3. Positive Connections:

Surrounding oneself with individuals who radiate positivity can have a profound impact. Positive relationships not only uplift spirits but also contribute to mutual growth and well-being.

4. Discernment:

Being discerning about the company we keep is important. Recognizing red flags such as habitual negativity or toxic behaviors can help safeguard against unnecessary drama and toxicity.

5. Wisdom of Analogy:

Understanding the analogy of sleeping akin to death serves as a guiding principle in discerning which relationships to nurture and which to let go of. It reminds us to choose our companions wisely and prioritize authenticity and mutual respect.

6. Balance:

Navigating relationships requires a delicate balance of acceptance and avoidance. By acknowledging people for who they truly are and making informed choices about our associations, we cultivate healthier, more fulfilling connections that enrich our lives.

Conclusion:

Navigating relationships is a journey that requires clarity, intention, and discernment. By prioritizing authenticity, positivity, and mutual respect, we pave the way for deeper, more meaningful connections that contribute to our overall well-being.

Chapter 15
Journey to Fulfillment Introduction

Achieving a fulfilling and purposeful life is a journey that involves distinct steps: isolation, insulation, revelation, transformation, and elevation. These stages are essential in personal growth and in realizing one's full potential. In this chapter, we will explore each step in detail, providing insights and practical advice on how to navigate this transformative journey.

Journey to Fulfillment

Isolation, insulation, revelation, transformation, and elevation. These are the steps to a fulfilling and purposeful life.

C R Wallace

Section 1: Isolation

Definition and Importance

Isolation is a phase of solitude and introspection, where one steps away from the distractions and noise of daily life to focus inward. This period is crucial for self-discovery, allowing individuals to reflect on their thoughts, emotions, and experiences without external influence.

Personal Experiences and Examples:

Consider the story of John, a successful but stressed-out executive who took a sabbatical to spend a month alone in a cabin. During this time, he reconnected with his passions and re-evaluated his life's direction. Historical figures like Henry David Thoreau, who retreated to Walden Pond, also exemplify the transformative power of isolation.

The Transformative Power of Isolation:

Consider the story of John, a successful but stressed-out executive who took a sabbatical to spend a month alone in a cabin. During this time, he reconnected with his passions and re-evaluated his life's direction. John's journey is a modern echo of historical figures like Henry David Thoreau, who retreated to Walden Pond, exemplifying the transformative power of isolation.

John's Journey to Self-Discovery:

John's life was a whirlwind of meetings, deadlines, and constant pressure. Despite his success, he felt a growing sense of dissatisfaction and burnout. Deciding to take a step back, John embarked on a month-long sabbatical in a remote cabin, disconnected from the relentless pace of his executive life.

In the stillness of the cabin, surrounded by nature, John experienced a profound shift. The quiet allowed him to reflect deeply on his life and priorities. He reconnected with hobbies he had long abandoned, such as painting and hiking, and found joy in simple, everyday activities. This period of solitude gave John the clarity to reassess his goals, ultimately leading him to make significant changes in his personal and professional life.

Henry David Thoreau and Walden Pond:

John's experience mirrors that of Henry David Thoreau, a 19th-century philosopher, naturalist, and author. Thoreau's retreat to Walden Pond is a seminal example of the transformative power of isolation. From 1845 to 1847, Thoreau lived in a small, self-built cabin by the pond in Concord, Massachusetts. His experiment in simple living was an intentional escape from the distractions and demands of society.

Thoreau's time at Walden Pond was not merely an escape but a deliberate act of self-exploration and intellectual inquiry. He chronicled his experiences in "Walden, or, Life in the Woods," reflecting on the virtues of simplicity, self-reliance, and the beauty of nature. Thoreau's writings have since inspired countless individuals to seek solitude as a means of gaining perspective and inner peace.

The Benefits of Solitude:

Both John's and Thoreau's stories highlight several benefits of solitude:

1. Mental Clarity: Time alone can help clear the mind of clutter, leading to better decision-making and problem-solving.

2. Emotional Healing: Isolation provides a space for emotional processing and healing from stress or trauma.

3. Creative Inspiration: Many find that solitude sparks creativity and new ideas, as distractions are minimized.

4. Personal Growth: Reflecting on one's life and goals in isolation can lead to significant personal development and changes in direction.

Applying These Lessons today:

In our fast-paced, hyper-connected world, the idea of retreating into solitude might seem impractical or even daunting. However, integrating periods of intentional isolation into our lives can offer profound benefits. Whether it's a weekend retreat, regular digital detoxes, or simply carving out time for solitary walks, finding ways to disconnect and reflect can lead to greater well-being and fulfillment.

John's sabbatical and Thoreau's retreat to Walden Pond serve as powerful reminders of the potential for transformation that lies in solitude. By embracing moments of isolation, we can reconnect with our true selves and navigate our lives with renewed clarity and purpose.

Practical Steps to incorporate isolation into your life:

Set aside regular time for solitude, whether it's a few hours a week or a weekend retreat. Create a peaceful environment free from digital distractions.

Use this time for activities like meditation, journaling, or simply being with your thoughts.

Section 2: Insulation

Definition and Importance of Insulation:

Insulation involves protecting oneself from negative influences and creating a supportive environment. Unlike isolation, which is about solitude, insulation is about selectively engaging with the world to maintain mental and emotional health. By effectively insulating oneself, individuals can foster a healthier, more positive mindset and achieve greater well-being.

Strategies for Insulation:

Effective insulation requires a thoughtful approach to interactions and environments. Here are key strategies:

1. **Identifying and Minimizing Exposure to Toxic Relationships and Environments:**

Recognize Negative Influences: The first step is identifying relationships or environments that drain energy, cause stress, or induce negativity. This could be a toxic work culture, unsupportive friends, or even certain social media platforms.

Limit Interaction: Once identified, minimize contact with these toxic elements. This might involve reducing time spent with certain individuals or avoiding specific settings altogether.

2. Establishing Healthy Boundaries:

Communicate Clearly: Clearly communicate your needs and limits to others. Let people know what behaviors are acceptable and which are not.

Be Assertive: Stand firm on your boundaries, even if it means facing opposition or discomfort. Your well-being should take precedence.

3. Building a Supportive Network of Positive Influences:

Cultivate Positive Relationships: Seek out and nurture relationships with individuals who uplift, support, and inspire you. These can be friends, family members, mentors, or colleagues.

Engage in Positive Environments: Spend time in environments that promote positivity and growth. This might include joining supportive communities, engaging in hobbies, or participating in activities that bring joy and fulfillment.

Case Studies

Sarah's Journey to Mental Health:

Consider Sarah, who realized that her social circle was draining her energy and causing stress. Surrounded by friends who were constantly negative and unsupportive, Sarah found herself feeling anxious and demotivated. Determined to improve her mental health, she took the following steps: Setting Boundaries: Sarah communicated her need for space and reduced her interactions with those who brought negativity into her life.

Seeking Positive Relationships: She sought out new friendships with individuals who shared her interests and values, finding support and encouragement in these new connections.

Engaging in Uplifting Activities: Sarah joined a local art class and a hiking group, both of which provided her with a sense of community and joy.

These changes significantly improved Sarah's mental health and reignited her motivation and enthusiasm for life.

Success through Supportive Environments:

Many successful people attribute their achievements to the supportive environments they cultivated. For instance, Entrepreneurs and Innovators: Steve Jobs famously emphasized the importance of surrounding himself with talented and creative individuals. His ability to insulate himself from naysayers and focus on positive, innovative influences was key to his success at Apple. Athletes: Professional athletes often speak about the crucial role of a supportive team, including coaches, family, and friends, in their journey to success. This network helps them stay focused, motivated, and resilient in the face of challenges.

Applying Insulation in Everyday Life:

To apply insulation in everyday life, consider the following practical steps:

1. Regular Self-Assessment: Periodically evaluate your relationships and environments to identify sources of negativity.

2. Proactive Boundary Setting: Don't wait for stress to build up. Proactively establish and communicate boundaries to maintain your well-being.

3. Active Network Building: Continuously seek out and invest in positive relationships and environments that support your growth and happiness.

By understanding and implementing the principles of insulation, individuals can protect their mental and emotional health, leading to a more balanced, fulfilling life.

Section 3: Revelation

Definition and Importance:

Revelation is the moment of gaining profound insight and clarity about oneself and one's purpose. This stage often follows periods of isolation and insulation, as the mind becomes more attuned to inner truths. Revelation is pivotal in personal development, offering transformative insights that can reshape one's direction and priorities.

Pathways to Revelation:

Revelations can be facilitated through several practices and experiences that encourage deep reflection and self-awareness:

1. Meditation and Mindfulness Practices:

Quieting the Mind: Regular meditation helps quiet the mind, reducing the noise of daily distractions. This mental stillness allows deeper insights to surface.

Enhancing Awareness: Mindfulness practices cultivate a heightened sense of awareness, helping individuals become more attuned to their thoughts, feelings, and surroundings. This increased awareness can lead to moments of profound clarity.

2. Journaling:

Processing Thoughts and Emotions: Writing regularly in a journal can help process and organize thoughts and emotions. This practice often leads to deeper self-understanding and can uncover hidden patterns or desires.

Reflecting on Experiences: Journaling provides a space to reflect on daily experiences and significant events, which can reveal underlying truths and insights about one's life path.

3. Engaging with Mentors, Books, and Experiences:

Mentors: Engaging with mentors who offer guidance and wisdom can provide new perspectives and challenge existing beliefs, fostering revelation.

Books: Reading books that inspire and challenge can introduce new ideas and stimulate profound reflections.

Experiences: Immersing oneself in new experiences, such as travel, workshops, or creative pursuits, can break routine patterns and open the mind to fresh insights.

Examples of Revelations:

Anna's Career Epiphany:

Consider the example of Anna, who spent months practicing meditation. Initially seeking stress relief, Anna soon found that her regular meditation sessions brought unexpected clarity. During one session, she had a sudden realization about her dissatisfaction with her current job. This revelation was profound, as it made her aware of her true passion for environmental conservation. Encouraged by this insight, Anna decided to pursue a career in this field, which brought her a deep sense of fulfillment and purpose.

Historical Example: Siddhartha Gautama

Historical figures like Siddhartha Gautama, who later became known as the Buddha, illustrate the power of revelation. Siddhartha's journey to enlightenment began with a deep dissatisfaction with his princely life and the suffering he observed in the world. He sought understanding through intense meditation and ascetic practices. After years of searching, Siddhartha experienced a profound revelation while meditating under the Bodhi tree. He attained enlightenment, gaining deep insights into the nature of suffering and the path to liberation. This revelation not only transformed his life but also laid the foundation for Buddhism, a major world religion.

Biblical Examples of Revelation

1. Moses and the Burning Bush:

Context: Moses encountered the burning bush in the wilderness while tending to his father-in-law's sheep.

Revelation: God revealed Himself to Moses, calling him to lead the Israelites out of slavery in Egypt. This profound moment of revelation gave Moses a clear sense of purpose and direction (Exodus 3).

2. Paul on the Road to Damascus:

Context: Saul, later known as Paul, was on his way to Damascus to persecute Christians when he experienced a life-changing revelation.

Revelation: A blinding light and the voice of Jesus confronted him, leading to his conversion and subsequent mission to spread Christianity (Acts 9:1-19).

3. John's Revelation on Patmos:

Context: John was exiled to the island of Patmos when he received a series of visions.

Revelation: These visions, documented in the Book of Revelation, provided profound insights into the future and the ultimate triumph of good over evil (Revelation 1:9-20).

Integrating Revelation into Daily Life

To integrate the concept of revelation into daily life, consider the following approaches:

1. Cultivate Regular Reflection:

Set aside time for meditation, mindfulness, or journaling to create opportunities for insights to emerge.

2. Seek Continuous Learning:

Engage with mentors, read thought-provoking books, and seek new experiences that challenge and inspire.

3. **Embrace Moments of Clarity:**

When revelations occur, honor them by reflecting deeply on their implications and considering how they can inform your life choices.

Revelation is a powerful stage in personal growth, offering the potential for transformative change. By creating the right conditions through practices like meditation, journaling, and engaging with inspirational sources, individuals can cultivate moments of profound insight that guide them toward a more authentic and fulfilling life.

Section 4: Transformation:

Definition and Importance:

Transformation is the process of internalizing revelations and making significant changes in one's life. This stage involves emotional, mental, and behavioral shifts that align with newfound insights. Transformation is crucial because it translates profound realizations into tangible actions and long-lasting changes, leading to a more authentic and fulfilling life.

Stages of Transformation:

Transformation often involves several interconnected stages:

1. **Emotional Adjustments:**

Letting Go of Past Traumas This involves healing from past experiences that have caused pain or hindered personal growth. It may include forgiving oneself or others and releasing negative emotions.

2. **Breaking Negative Patterns**:

Recognizing and breaking free from recurring negative behaviors or thought patterns is essential. This can involve confronting fears, overcoming self-doubt, and embracing a more positive outlook.

3. **Mental Shifts:**

Adopting New Beliefs and Attitudes: Transformation often requires a shift in mindset. This can mean embracing new philosophies, values, or perspectives that align with one's revelations. It involves letting go of limiting beliefs and adopting a more open and growth-oriented mindset. Enhancing Self-Awareness: Developing a deeper understanding of oneself and one's motivations is crucial. This self-awareness helps in making informed decisions that align with one's true purpose.

4. **Behavioral Changes:**

Pursuing New Goals: Transformation leads to setting new, meaningful goals that reflect one's insights and aspirations. This might involve changing careers, starting new projects, or embarking on personal ventures.

Altering Daily Routines: Small, consistent changes in daily habits and routines can support the larger transformation. This might include incorporating new practices like exercise, meditation, or creative activities that reinforce the new direction.

Success Stories Marcus' Transformation Journey

Consider the transformation of Marcus, who worked in a high-paying but unfulfilling corporate job. Over time, Marcus realized his true passion was teaching and making a difference in the lives of young people. After much reflection and planning, he decided to leave his corporate position to start an educational non-profit.

Emotional Adjustment:

Marcus had to let go of the security and identity tied to his corporate role. He also confronted his fears about financial stability and societal expectations.

Mental Shifts:

He adopted a new belief in the value of education and his ability to effect change. This shift empowered him to see his work as meaningful and impactful.

Behavioral Changes:

Marcus pursued his new goal by gaining relevant qualifications, networking with educators, and building his non-profit from the ground up. He altered his daily routines to include teaching, fundraising, and program development.

Marcus' story demonstrates how transformation, fueled by revelation, can lead to a more purposeful and satisfying life.

Biblical Examples of Transformation:

1. Saul to Paul:

Context: Saul, a fervent persecutor of Christians, experienced a profound revelation on the road to Damascus. Transformation: After his revelation, Saul became Paul, one of the most influential apostles in Christianity. His emotional adjustment involved repenting for his past actions, his mental shift included embracing the teachings of Jesus, and his behavioral change was his lifelong mission to spread Christianity (Acts 9).

2. Zacchaeus:

Context: Zacchaeus, a wealthy tax collector, had an encounter with Jesus that changed his life.

Transformation: Following his interaction with Jesus, Zacchaeus decided to give half of his possessions to the poor and repay those he had cheated on fourfold. This transformation involved emotional repentance, a mental shift in understanding justice and generosity, and behavioral changes in how he managed his wealth and interactions with others (Luke 19:1-10).

3. Peter:

Context: Peter, one of Jesus' disciples, experienced several transformative moments, particularly after Jesus' resurrection.

Transformation:

Peter's transformation involves overcoming his fear and guilt from denying Jesus three times. His mental shift came from understanding his role in the early church, and his behavioral change was seen in his leadership and preaching, eventually becoming a pillar of the Christian community (John 21:15-19, Acts 2).

Integrating Transformation into Daily Life:

To integrate the concept of transformation into daily life, consider these approaches:

1. Embrace Continuous Learning and Growth:

Regularly seek out new knowledge and experiences that challenge and inspire you.

2. Reflect and Adapt:

Periodically assess your emotional, mental, and behavioral states to ensure they align with your goals and values.

3. Implement Small Changes:

Make incremental adjustments to your daily routines and habits that support your broader transformation.

Transformation is an ongoing process that requires commitment and self-awareness. By embracing emotional adjustments, mental shifts, and behavioral changes, individuals can transform their lives in meaningful ways, aligning with their true purpose and achieving greater fulfillment.

Section 5: Elevation:

Definition and Importance:

Elevation is the culmination of the journey, where one reaches a higher state of being and purpose. This stage is marked by a sense of fulfillment and a clear direction in life.

Achieving Elevation:

To achieve and maintain elevation:

- Cultivate daily practices that promote well-being and growth, such as exercise, meditation, and continuous learning. Focus on self-improvement and embracing new challenges.

Impact of Elevation:

Elevation results in a more fulfilling and purposeful life. Elevated individuals often make significant contributions to their communities and inspire others through their actions. Examples include figures like Nelson Mandela, whose elevated state of being led to profound societal impact.

Conclusion:

In summary, the journey to a fulfilling and purposeful life involves the steps of isolation, insulation, revelation, transformation, and elevation. Each stage is essential for personal growth and achieving one's full potential. Remember, this journey is cyclical and ongoing, encouraging continuous development and fulfillment. Embrace these steps, and embark on your own path to a meaningful life.

Reflection Questions and Exercises:

Reflection Questions:

1. What areas of your life require isolation for deeper reflection?

2. Who or what do you need to insulate yourself from to protect your well-being?

3. What practices can you incorporate to facilitate personal revelations?

4. How can you transform your life based on recent insights?

5. What daily habits can help you maintain an elevated state of being?

Practical Exercises:

1. Schedule a weekly "solitude time" for self-reflection.

2. Write a list of toxic influences in your life and develop a plan to minimize their impact.

3. Start a daily journal to track your thoughts and revelations.

4. Set a transformative goal based on a recent revelation and outline actionable steps to achieve it.

5. Establish a routine that includes practices promoting elevation, such as mindfulness, exercise, and learning.

Chapter 16

Navigating Life's Traffic Lights: Recognizing and Responding to Emotional Signals

Guiding Lights of Life "Navigating life's pathway to our destiny requires understanding and obeying emotional signals, which protect us from hazards. This is similar to how traffic signals ensure our safety on the road."

C.R. Wallace

Introduction:

Imagine driving without paying attention to traffic lights. Ignoring red, amber, or green lights can lead to accidents and chaos. Similarly, in life, ignoring emotional signals can be dangerous. These signals often serve as warnings or guides, helping us navigate through complex situations and relationships. Ignoring them can lead to emotional distress, unresolved conflicts, and even mental health issues. It's crucial to pay attention to these signals, just as we do with traffic lights.

Driving through an intersection without heeding traffic lights is a recipe for disaster. Red lights demand a full stop, amber lights urge caution, and green lights signal it's safe to proceed. Each light plays a crucial role in ensuring the smooth and safe flow of traffic. Ignoring these signals could result in accidents, causing harm to ourselves and others.

In the same way, our emotions act as internal traffic lights. Red emotions like anger, fear, or sadness signal us to stop and reflect. They often indicate that something is wrong and needs addressing. Amber emotions, such as unease or apprehension, advise us to proceed with caution, suggesting that we need to pay attention to potential problems or conflicts. Green emotions, like joy and contentment, encourage us to move forward, embracing positive experiences and interactions.

Just as driving recklessly through a red light can lead to crashes, ignoring our emotional 'red lights' can result in significant turmoil. Suppressing feelings of anger, fear, or sadness doesn't make them disappear; instead, they fester and grow, leading to increased stress and potential mental health issues like anxiety or depression. Similarly, neglecting the amber warnings of our emotions can cause us to overlook important signs that something needs to change, leading to unresolved conflicts and strained relationships.

On the other hand, paying attention to our emotional signals allows us to navigate life's complexities more effectively. By acknowledging and addressing our red-light emotions, we can take steps to resolve underlying issues, seek support, and promote healing. By heeding our amber-light emotions, we can approach situations with the necessary caution and awareness, preventing potential problems from escalating. And by embracing our green light emotions, we can fully experience and appreciate the positive aspects of our lives, fostering happiness and well-being.

Just as drivers rely on traffic lights to guide them safely on the road, we must rely on our emotional signals to guide us through life's journey. By paying attention to these internal cues, we can maintain emotional balance, enhance our relationships, and promote overall mental health. Ignoring them, however, can lead to chaos and distress, much like ignoring traffic lights leads to accidents on the road.

Ignoring the Signals is Dangerous:

Picture yourself at a busy intersection. The traffic lights change from green to amber, then to red. You know what each color signifies and act accordingly to ensure your safety and the safety of others. Now, consider your emotional life. Emotional signals are just as critical, yet we often overlook them.

Ignoring these signals can be perilous. Just as running a red light can lead to a crash, ignoring emotional red flags can result in severe emotional distress, strained relationships, and long-term mental health issues. Paying attention to these signals is crucial for maintaining emotional well-being and navigating life's challenges effectively.

Understanding Amber, Red, and Hazard Lights:

To understand emotional signals better, let's use the analogy of traffic lights:

Amber Light: Caution:

Amber lights in traffic signal caution – slow down and prepare to stop. Similarly, an amber light in your emotional life suggests something needs your attention. It might be a subtle hint that something is off or a situation that requires careful consideration. For instance, if you feel uneasy in a conversation or notice a change in someone's behavior, take a moment to evaluate what's happening. These caution signals help you avoid potential issues before they escalate.

Neglecting these signals can be perilous. Just as running a red light can lead to a collision, ignoring emotional red flags can result in profound emotional distress, strained relationships, and enduring mental health challenges. Giving attention to these signals is essential for sustaining emotional well-being and effectively navigating life's complexities.

When you encounter emotional "red lights," such as feelings of intense anger, overwhelming sadness, or profound fear, they serve as warnings. Ignoring them can allow tensions to escalate, potentially damaging relationships and triggering internal turmoil. Addressing these emotions with introspection, communication, or seeking support can prevent escalation and foster emotional resilience.

Similarly, emotional "amber lights" signal caution. These may include feelings of unease, discomfort, or uncertainty in certain situations or relationships. Recognizing these signals prompts thoughtful consideration and proactive measures to address underlying concerns before they exacerbate into larger issues.

Conversely, emotional "green lights," such as feelings of joy, contentment, and fulfillment, indicate positive experiences and emotional alignment. Embracing and nurturing these emotions contributes to overall well-being and strengthens emotional connections with others.

Just as you intuitively respond to traffic signals for physical safety, tuning into emotional signals safeguards your psychological health. It allows you to navigate life's challenges with greater resilience, maintain healthier relationships, and foster a deeper understanding of yourself. By respecting and responding to your emotional signals, you empower yourself to lead a more balanced and fulfilling life.

Red Light: Stop:

Red lights mean stop immediately. In your emotional life,

red lights are strong warnings to halt and reassess the situation. These could be instances of manipulation, gas lighting, or projecting. If you consistently feel drained, anxious, or doubt your reality, it's a red light. Such toxic behaviors significantly impact your mental health, and recognizing these signals is crucial to protect yourself.

By understanding and respecting these emotional traffic lights, you can navigate life's challenges more effectively and maintain healthier relationships. Stay safe, stay aware, and always wait for the green light before proceeding.

Hazard Lights: Immediate Action:

Hazard lights indicate danger and the need for immediate action. If you're overwhelmed or in a situation where you're constantly manipulated or gaslighted, it's time to turn on your hazard lights. This is your signal to seek help, set boundaries, and protect yourself from harm. Recognizing these severe warning signs can prevent further emotional damage and guide you to safety.

Green Light: Proceed with Joy:

Green lights in traffic signify that it is safe to proceed. In our emotional lives, green lights symbolize positive emotions such as joy, contentment, and excitement. These emotions indicate that things are going well and it's safe to continue on your current path. Embracing these green light moments allows you to fully experience the good times in life, reinforcing positive behaviors and fostering a sense of well-being.

Green light emotions are essential for mental health as they encourage us to keep moving forward, engaging with life and others in a meaningful way. When you experience feelings of happiness, fulfillment, or satisfaction, take the time to appreciate and savor these moments. They are indicators that you are on the right track and that your efforts and decisions are leading to positive outcomes.

Cultivating more green light moments involves being mindful of what brings you joy and actively seeking out these experiences. This might include spending time with loved ones, pursuing hobbies and interests, or simply taking a moment to enjoy the beauty of nature. By recognizing and embracing green light emotions, you can enhance your overall well-being and resilience.

Personal Experience and Recognition:

I've encountered amber lights recently, signaling caution. It's a familiar scene for me, one I've seen before. Recognizing these early warning signals helps me take preventive measures. Reflecting on past experiences, we can identify patterns and signs indicating when something isn't right. This awareness is crucial for maintaining emotional health and avoiding potentially harmful situations.

Manipulation, Gas lighting, and Projecting:

Let's delve into three toxic behaviors often signaled by our emotional traffic lights: Manipulation: This involves controlling or influencing someone deceptively. Recognizing manipulation is like spotting an amber light – it calls for caution and awareness. Being aware of manipulative tactics can help you avoid being deceived and maintain healthy relationships.

Gas lighting:

This is when someone makes you doubt your reality or sanity. It's a red light situation, requiring you to stop and reassess the relationship or situation. Gas lighting can be incredibly damaging, leading to severe self-doubt and confusion. Recognizing it early is essential for protecting your mental health.

Projecting:

This occurs when someone attributes their own negative traits or feelings to you. It can be confusing and damaging, often necessitating the use of your emotional hazard lights to protect yourself. Understanding this behavior helps you maintain clarity and avoid internalizing someone else's issues.

Conclusion:

Recognizing and responding to emotional signals is essential for our well-being. Just as we obey traffic lights to ensure safety on the roads, we must heed these emotional signals to navigate life effectively. Pay attention to your feelings and intuitions, and don't hesitate to seek help or set boundaries when necessary. Remember, ignoring these signals can be dangerous.

By understanding and respecting these emotional traffic lights, you can navigate life's challenges more effectively and maintain healthier relationships. Stay safe, stay aware, and always wait for the green light before proceeding.

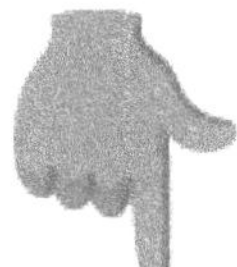

Key Takeaways:

1. Emotional Signals as Guides:

Emotions serve as internal traffic lights, guiding us through life's complexities.

Ignoring these signals can lead to emotional distress and mental health issues.

2. Red Light Emotions:

Red emotions like anger, fear, and sadness signal a need to stop and reflect.

Addressing these emotions can prevent escalation and promote healing.

3. Amber Light Emotions:

Amber emotions, such as unease and apprehension, indicate caution is needed.

Recognizing these signals allows proactive measures to avoid potential problems.

4. Green Light Emotions:

Green emotions like joy and contentment encourage moving forward and embracing positive experiences.

Cultivating and savoring green light moments enhances overall well-being.

5. Hazard Lights:

Hazard lights indicate immediate danger and the need for urgent action.

In situations of manipulation, gas lighting, or projecting, seeking help and setting boundaries is crucial.

6. Personal Awareness:

Reflecting on past experiences helps identify patterns and early warning signs.

Awareness of these signals is vital for maintaining emotional health and avoiding harmful situations.

7. Toxic Behaviors:

Recognizing manipulation, gas lighting, and projecting

helps maintain clarity and protect mental health.

Early recognition of these behaviors allows for appropriate action to be taken.

8. Mindful Engagement:

Paying attention to and respecting emotional signals leads to better decision-making and healthier relationships.

Mindful engagement with emotions fosters resilience and deeper self-understanding.

9. Balancing Emotions:

Just as traffic lights ensure safety on the roads, emotional signals help maintain emotional balance.

Heeding these signals enhances overall mental health and life satisfaction.

About The Author

Clarence R. Wallace is a thoughtful and introspective author dedicated to exploring the deeper meanings of life and the nourishment of the human soul. With a profound understanding of spiritual wisdom, Wallace delves into the timeless truths that guide us toward inner peace, love, and fulfillment.

In his book, "Nourishment For The Soul: Quotes He Wrote," Wallace draws from a rich tapestry of personal experiences and scriptural insights, weaving them into compelling narratives that challenge readers to look beyond the superficial trappings of material wealth and success. His writing is marked by its eloquence and a deep-seated passion for helping others discover the true essence of spiritual well-being.

Wallace's work is not just a collection of words, but a heartfelt invitation to embark on a transformative journey of self-discovery and spiritual growth. Through his carefully crafted prose, he encourages readers to reflect on their own lives, urging them to prioritize the nourishment of their souls in a world often consumed by the pursuit of material gain.

Clarence R. Wallace's dedication to the principles of love, compassion, and inner tranquility shines through in his writing, making him a beacon of light for those seeking to enrich their lives spiritually. His insightful reflections and practical wisdom offer guidance and inspiration, making "Nourishment For The Soul" a must-read for anyone yearning for a deeper connection with their innermost self.